CU00839389

UN-STABLE LANE

Julie Round

OLDSTICK BOOKS

First Published in Great Britain in 2009 by
Oldstick Books
18 Wiston Close
Worthing
BN14 7PU

Copyright © 2009 Julie Round

Names, characters and related indicia are copyright and trademark
Copyright © 2009 Julie Round

Julie Round has asserted her moral rights
to be identified as the author

A CIP Catalogue of this book is available from
the British Library

ISBN 978-0-9557242-1-3

All rights reserved; no part of this publication may be reproduced or
transmitted by any means, electronic, mechanical, photocopying
or otherwise without the written permission of the publisher.

Cover Photos: ©istockphoto.com/

Portrait Photograph by David Sawyer
www.the-photographer.org.

Typeset in Garamond 12pt
by Chandler Book Design,
www.chandlerbookdesign.co.uk

Printed in Great Britain by the
MPG Books Group, Bodmin and King's Lynn.

To Mum and Dad
with gratitude.

1

"Quick – grab a round table for four," Tania called as Katie stood, bewildered, in the doorway.

The place was entirely different from what she had expected. It looked like a plush cinema with fancy soft carpet and concealed lighting.

There were fruit machines round the walls and a snack bar in the corner with a set of stairs leading up to another floor. The carpet was rich blue with bold yellow and red stars and everywhere gleamed red and gold.

"I'll get your books, Katie. You can buy a dabber from the diner if you don't want to use a pen," called Sally.

She felt rushed and nervous as she sat by the large table. Most of the people were seated at curved booths which snaked across the lower floor, each with their own seats and complicated looking displays. Here, from a raised section of the room, Katie could see that there were a surprising number of men. Why had she thought only women played Bingo? The age group was unexpected, too. All ages from 20 to 90 were represented and there

1

was a great deal of chatter and laughter, as if it was a social club.

"Five pounds a line, Fifteen pounds a full house," came a voice over the loudspeaker.

What was she doing here? she wondered. Perhaps it was a reaction to her father's funeral – a belated rebellion. She hadn't been able to defy him while he was alive, had she? So she was doing it now he was dead. But there was more to it than that.

Her life had changed in so many ways since she had married. Yet she still felt her father's presence in the house they shared with her mother.

When she and Ned had first moved in Katie was fearful that her mother would take over the care of Heather, their two year old daughter, but once Katie joined the mother and baby club she felt better. She found new friends with similar experiences. Tania and Sally could hardly be more different yet, in their company, Katie felt accepted and appreciated.

Tania had hit the nail on the head when she'd asked how Katie had enjoyed herself before she was married. If she didn't go into pubs, had she gone to gigs or parties, or just gone shopping?

Katie had done none of these things. Tania had scoffed and made her feel an old woman before her time. Of course she would never have wanted to lead the kind of life Tania had – drifting from one rave to another, living in squats and sleeping with a succession of different men, one of whom left her with a son and disappeared back to Scotland with no forwarding address. Tania's latest partner was Duane, who worked as a security guard. They rented a house on the edge of the village and, although they weren't married, it seemed a long-term arrangement.

It was Sally who had persuaded Katie to come tonight; tall, elegant Sally with her long, blonde hair and her perfect marriage. If she thought Bingo was an acceptable way to spend an evening then Katie felt it must be OK.

Katie had been surprised and flattered that they had asked her to join them for a night out - until she realised that they hoped she would drive them into town. She didn't really mind. She liked to feel needed and it was an opportunity to do something she had never done before.

When Katie first took her daughter, Heather, to the village playgroup it was Sally and her 3 year old daughter Emily who immediately made them feel at home.

The more she found out about Sally the more she envied the life she seemed to have with her husband, one of complete trust and understanding.

"Don't you ever argue?" she'd asked her friend.

"Well – we have differences of opinion, but once we work out why we think differently we can usually come to a compromise."

Katie was amazed. Neither her parents, nor she and Ned, ever tried to work out why they disagreed. Her mother used to give in to her father and she realised, guiltily, that Ned, her husband, usually followed her suggestions. But then Ned was slow, slow to learn, slow to react and slow to understand. Ever since they met, Katie had always been the leader, which was fine by her – at least, most of the time.

Even so, she'd been happy to leave Heather at home with him while she worked at the care home. It was only after the toddler had been taken away from them because Ned had been considered an unsuitable parent, and they had been forced to accept her mother's offer to move in with her in order to get their child back, that she began to resent the fact that Ned and her mother saw more of Heather than she did. Not only that - they seemed to have a connection that she could not penetrate. Rose seemed to know what Ned was thinking even when he didn't say anything. Their partnership in running the smallholding had blossomed as they planned the camping site. They both seemed happy, excited and fulfilled. That was it, those were the feelings that were missing from her life and she didn't think Friday night at Bingo was going to provide them.

"You've got six," whispered Tania, looking over her shoulder. They had started calling and she had been daydreaming. How could she have missed the numbers as they were flashed up on giant screens?

"Two and one, twenty one." The voice was loud and clear. Katie tried to concentrate. It wasn't easy, knowing Tania was watching her.

"Seven O, seventy." She'd got that too, but someone was already calling out that they had a line. Katie looked round at the other players. They all looked so absorbed. She just could not get enthusiastic about spending time this way.

The game ended and Sally began taking orders for food. "We can have it down here or finish our five games and eat upstairs," she explained. "How do you feel?"

"Five games will be enough for me," replied Katie. "What's upstairs?"

"It's just a bar-but it is quieter. We usually go up but Tania wants to play the big game. Here, have a look at the menu and I'll order now."

Katie took the menu and scanned the choices. "A bacon and mushroom panini sounds nice."

"Great. If I rush I'll be back for the next game," and

she forged between the tables towards the corner of the hall.

Katie looked up above the screens and fruit machines and saw that one side of the room was an enormous glass window. Shadowy shapes moved in and out of view but it was difficult to hold her head at that angle and when the music stopped and the lights changed she tried to focus on her page of numbers.

She had four numbers left to find when the game ended. She was ready to have her supper and go home.

The upper level was every bit as plush as the downstairs. The carpet was thick, the décor was muted and the lighting was discreet. People were sitting or standing, talking quietly. It seemed altogether more civilised than she had anticipated and she began to relax.

"Hi, Sally," called out a man at the bar, "Where's Jess?"

"She couldn't make it tonight, Cam. – Katie brought us."

"Hallo, Katie." The man came nearer and his companions turned to look at her.

"I'm Cameron. This is Al and that's Blogger."

Katie's eyes skimmed over a man in a leather jacket to a big, bald, barrel-chested giant who gave her a cheesy grin.

Cameron was asking, "What do you think of the place?"

"It's quite nice." Katie felt like a schoolgirl. She'd never been the centre of attention before and she felt herself blushing. Luckily Cameron, the introductions over, turned to Sally.

"Win anything tonight?"

"No luck – but Tania's still hopeful. We left her down there."

They all stared through the window, one man leaning over Katie to get a better look.

"Hey!" she exclaimed, "Don't squash me."

"Sorry, love. I didn't think."

It was Al. His open jacket had fallen across her face.

"If you just shove up a bit I'll sit down and then I won't be in your way."

"Number 22," called a voice and Sally replied, "Here," and waved a wooden spoon with the number on that had been in the centre of the table.

"Mmm – that looks good," commented Al. "How about some chips, lads?" and he left the table.

Katie gave a sigh of relief. Now she could eat her panini in peace. Why was Sally grinning at her so knowingly?

"You're in there, Katie."

"Don't be stupid. He was just being polite."

Sally sighed, but said no more.

Katie had hardly finished her meal when there was a flurry of movement from downstairs. Someone was jumping up and down and people were patting her on the back.

"It must be the prize winner from the group game," muttered Sally. "Can you see who it is?"

"The window is misty – but I think it could be Tania. I do hope it is."

"Let's go and find out," but they only got as far as the door when they met Tania coming up.

"Five hundred pounds! I've won five hundred pounds," she shouted.

"Don't tell the world," laughed Sally. "Well done, Tania. What are you going to do with it?"

"Spend it, of course," Tania chuckled. "Can I get you both a drink?

"Too late," said the barman. "The lads have already got you girls something to celebrate with." He put down a tray with a large bottle of champagne and four glasses.

Sally moved across to let Tania have a seat. Immediately the three men crowded round the end of the table and Katie felt Al sit down next to her again.

"You don't mind, do you?" he smiled.

"No," she muttered, but she was intensely aware of his leg against hers and dare not move away in case he felt insulted. The glasses were being filled and Sally declared, "A toast – to Tania"

"To Tania," they all chorused and the men rang their beer glasses together.

Katie took a peek at Al's profile. He reminded her of someone. Who was it? An athlete – oh yes, that famous runner who became a politician. He felt her gaze and turned and smiled at her. "What are you thinking?"

"Oh, I'm just enjoying the champagne," she lied.

Sally helped herself to another glass. She was flushed and talking loudly, giggling at her own jokes. Tania had vanished. Katie felt uncomfortable.

"Where's Tania?" she asked.

"She's gone off with Cameron," replied Al. "Don't worry – she knows him. He'll see her home."

Katie was ready to leave. She shifted awkwardly in her seat.

"I think it's time we went," she said.

"You'll come again next week?"

"If the girls need a lift. It's been quite a change."

Al stood to let her out and gave a little bow. She laughed. He really did look rather nice and she felt

7

flattered that he'd singled her out for attention.

It seemed odd going home without Tania but Sally obviously thought it was unremarkable. Katie dropped her off in the village and drove back along Stable Lane, turning left past the camping site and again up Chalk Pit Lane to Lane's End and the garage.

There was a light in the kitchen of the house. Was someone waiting up for her?

It was her mother.

Katie closed the porch door behind her, suppressing the thought that she was being treated more like a teenager than a married woman.

"Hallo, dear. Did you have a nice time?" Rose pulled her dressing gown round her and placed an empty mug in the sink.

"Yes thanks, Mum. Although it made me think how angry father would have been if he'd known I was gambling."

"As long as you enjoyed yourself. Heather was as good as gold. Night, love. See you in the morning."

Katie felt restless. She should go up to bed. Hopefully, Ned would be asleep – but she needed a few moments to wind down. She hoped Jessica's car was still out of action next week and she could go again. She couldn't remember when she had last felt so alive!

Rose woke early to the sound of birdsong. She should feel content, she thought. It was Saturday. More people were coming to the camp site. The shop was up and running and her family were healthy, happy and all around her.

Yet her ex-husband's funeral had put a cloud over the week. Perhaps that was what felt wrong – the 'ex.' She'd never got used to being divorced. She had been forced to do it. With Tim in prison it was the only way to convince everyone that Lane's End was a safe place for her granddaughter.

But it had surprised her that he had chosen, and paid for, a woodland burial. She knew, of course, that he wasn't religious and now she came to think of it there were only two things he'd really loved – his dog, Jenny, and the land. So she supposed it made sense for him to be buried in the most natural way.

Katie had not attended the funeral. She had insisted on staying home with Heather. The only other people there were George, Tim's brother, his wife Pat and Rose's son-in-law.

When Rose got downstairs Bernard was already sat on the floor of the lounge with Heather. They had emptied out the box of bricks and Bernard was lining them up in a row.

Rose began to get breakfast and had just laid the table when Katie came down with an armful of bedding. "I'll just put these in the machine, OK, Mum? I've stripped the bed and left the clean sheets out for Bernard to make the bed."

Rose winced. Katie usually called her husband Ned and only called Bernard by his real name when she was disappointed with him. What had the poor man done, or not done, now?

As soon as breakfast was over Katie said, "Come on, Heather, let's go and see if the chickens have left any eggs."

Bernard did not seem to notice that he was being ignored and wandered back to the sitting room. He had a piece of paper and a crayon and had laid the bricks out to spell B LOGMAN but Rose could see that he was not satisfied.

"That's almost your name, isn't it, Bernard?"

"Yes, but there's something missing."

"It's another N. You've used one but you need another one, after the O."

Bernard turned over the bricks until he found the missing letter. "I'm going to try to write to Zak," he said. "He promised to come and see us."

"That's great – but we have new people coming today. Can you bring some things down to the camp site for me?"

"Sure. I'll just put these away," and he stacked the bricks neatly into their box.

When Rose reached the shop Pat was already there, although they had agreed her hours should be eleven until one and four till six. She'd worked much longer hours as a licensee and, as she and George were renting the shop, could come and go when she liked.

A large blue 4x4 turned in from the lane and stopped outside the office. Rose slid the window open and called out.

"Good morning. Mr and Mrs Telford? Pitch number four. Here's a map of the layout. You may park by the hedge on the left. We don't allow vehicles on the rest of the field. The shop is open until one in case you need anything. I hope you have a pleasant stay."

She heard Pat giggle behind her. "You sound so in command," she commented.

"I should do. I had guests in the house for years. Now – how about a cup of coffee?"

Pat's ample bosom still shook as she filled the kettle.

"How did Katie enjoy the Bingo?"

"She didn't say." Rose turned her chair to face the

table. "I don't like it, Pat. I know she needs to get out and enjoy herself but I would rather it was with Bernard than with those women."

Rose knew how little time Katie had spent with people of her own age. If only she had stood up to Tim and encouraged her daughter to go out more.

"They don't do anything silly, do they? They all have children," said Pat.

"That doesn't mean they're all married."

Perhaps she was old-fashioned but she was unhappy with her daughter's burgeoning friendship with Tania. A mother who lived with one man while openly going out with another was not a good example.

"Katie wouldn't stray. She adores Bernard."

Pat was echoing Rose's own fears, but she wouldn't admit it. Instead, she came to Katie's defence.

"She loves him all right – but like you love a big, cuddly toy. I don't think she respects him. She used to – when he made the mosaics and was called Ned, the artist, but since he's turned to market gardening she seems to have lost that feeling."

"That's because of Tim. It's sub-conscious. I'm sure it will be OK. It does us girls good to flirt a bit but most of us know which side our bread is buttered!"

It wasn't just flirting that Rose was concerned about – it was knowing how drink changed people's characters and freed them from inhibitions. She didn't want Katie to do anything she would regret, or that would hurt Bernard.

The bell on the shop counter rang and Pat hurried out of the office. Rose closed the window and went through the shop and into the courtyard.

There were buildings on three sides, the shop nearest the road, then the computer repair centre and the craft shop and, opposite her, the washrooms and toilets for the camp. Bernard had wandered across to the units.

"What are you looking for, Bernard?"

"I wish I could make something like the things in the shop."

"Chantelle isn't in yet - but when she is, you could ask her."

Rose wasn't sure that the craft shop was the ideal occupant for their units – but it was a new local business and she had warmed to the young owner. Chantelle's home-made cards and trinkets, cushions and toys were attractive enough – but there was no passing trade and she had to rely on mail order. Chantelle herself was an intriguing and persuasive saleswoman, with long dark hair, a heart-shaped face and a size 22 figure. Yet her fingers were delicate and nimble. Rose had watched her threading beads and sewing.

Being next to a computer shop with printing facilities delighted Chantelle. Rose, too, thought this was the perfect tenant. About Computers had two vans which seemed to be zipping in and out of the complex at all times of the day and night.

"We'd better get back, Bernard. Lunch is at twelve. Katie has to be at work at two."

"Yes. I'm coming." He looked thoughtful as he turned away.

"We found five eggs, Nana," Heather called out as they entered the kitchen. "Mummy said we could make Yorkshire pudding tomorrow."

"That's a good idea, darling. Where's Mummy now?"

"I was putting the washing out." Katie had followed them in. "I'll just go up and change my shoes."

She didn't acknowledge her husband and the smile that had lit up his face when he saw her died. Katie was in one of her moods. Rose knew better than to question her. She just hoped she would get over it soon.

Bernard spent the afternoon mowing the front lawn. He was used to Katie's odd shifts and had been asleep when she came to bed the previous night. He'd woken with her familiar warmth against his back and rolled over carefully to cuddle her. Her hair was longer, now – the unruly dark curls flicked out below her ears, her pixie face at rest. He loved the sight of her asleep, even more than when she laughed – but she didn't laugh much these days. She was always so rushed and busy. He'd hoped, with the three of them to look after Heather, life would be more relaxed, but nothing ever seemed perfect.

He put the mower away in the garage and strolled down to the camp site.

Pat was serving a customer so he waited until they had left and then perched on a stool by the counter watching her, red hair gleaming, as she bent to count the takings.

"Not much doing today, Bernard," she said, "Mostly bread and milk," and then she chuckled. "Not together, of course."

Bernard grinned. He liked Pat. She seemed to make everything fun. When she'd been a landlady she had laughed and joked with all the customers. Now she was on her own a lot while George was away driving but she still never looked sad or troubled.

"Your friend will be visiting soon, won't he?" she asked.

"Zak? Yes. I'm trying to write more so that I can send him letters."

"That's great. I really admire you, Bernard. You never stop trying, do you?"

Bernard was about to reply when there was a deafening roar followed by some strange popping noises outside the shop.

"Oh, no," said Pat.

"What is it?"

"Motorbikes."

Bernard went to the doorway and looked out. Six large motorbikes had drawn up in the courtyard. The riders all wore black, although some of their helmets had orange flames and other coloured designs on them.

One rider had dismounted and took off his helmet. His bearded face looked ghostly in the evening light.

Bernard blocked the way into the shop. He tried not to show the fear he felt. There were too many for him to tackle. He hoped Pat was on the phone for help.

"Hi,Bernard," growled the man.

"Do I know you?"

"Frank – one of Craig's mates. Is his mum in?"

Pat pushed past Bernard and embraced Frank. "You old trouble-maker. What do you want now?"

"We're after a favour, Pat. We'd like you to put up a few friends from up north. There's a rally at the Heritage Centre one weekend but they'd like to spend a few days here. How about it?"

"I'd have to ask Rose but if you'll vouch for them it should be OK. No wild parties or barbeques, though."

Bernard remembered then. These had been the people who came to the pub when Pat's son had been behind the

14

bar. They had witnessed his fatal accident. They might look frightening but they were a friendly crowd. It was just their machines that were so loud and threatening.

"Have you got any beer, Pat?" came a shout from another rider.

"No, sorry, love – no licence – plenty of coke."

A girl's voice called out, "Naughty, naughty," and they all laughed.

"Anyway, I'm clearing up now. I've got Rachel's number. I'll let you know what Rose says. What are the dates?"

"Last Wednesday in July. Three tents, five people."

"We'll let you know. Take care."

"Fine," responded Frank. "Ta-ra, folks," and with an explosion of revs they were gone.

Bernard looked round for Pat. She had gone back inside the shop. The light in the office was on and he pushed open the door.

Pat was sitting at the desk, crying.

"What's the matter, Pat?"

"Oh, Bernard, I'm such a silly old thing. It was just seeing the bikes. I kept thinking Craig should be with them."

Bernard felt helpless. "Come and see Rose," was the only suggestion he could make and Pat dried her eyes and nodded. They packed up and walked the long way round to the cottage. Neither fancied going through the fields or the orchard in the gloom.

Rose had made warm, thick soup and home-made bread for them all. Heather was in bed and after supper Rose drove Pat to the houseboat.

Bernard sat alone in the silent house. He did not like seeing anyone unhappy, least of all the women in his life. It had been easy to make Pat feel better. Rose had listened

15

while Pat remembered happier times she had spent with her son and then moved the conversation on to the present and how much Pat was needed and admired. He could see by the time she left Pat was calm and content.

He wished he could work such a miracle with Katie. How could he show her how special she was to him? He wanted to make her something – something precious and glittering, jewellery fit for a princess. He would ask Chantelle to teach him how to make a really fancy necklace.

He felt more confident once he had made his decision. Katie would be back soon and he would make them both some cocoa and tell her about the motorbike boys.

He wished she wasn't always so tired when she came home.

The following Wednesday Katie felt unusually excited. She bumped the empty pushchair over the rough ground in the orchard and then, when they reached the road, plonked a protesting Heather into it and trotted briskly to the hall.

She was one of the first mums there and had to help put out the tiny chairs and tables and unroll the blanket for the babies to play on. Outside this protective square the toddlers were given space to play with push-along toys, trikes, rocking horses, prams and, in the next room, books and a doll's house.

Once Sally had arrived with Emily, Katie could wait no longer.

"Is Jess coming?" she asked.

"Oh, no. The car's fixed but they always go away in June so that they miss the school holidays."

"So you'll want a lift on Friday?"

"Yes, please. We enjoyed having you with us."

Katie glowed. That was what she wanted to hear. She couldn't have put into words the difference just one night out in company had made to her life. Now she had something to look forward to.

The music seemed louder- the place warmer and her hands stickier as she dabbed away at the numbers. For a moment she thought she was going to win a line, but it was not to be.

She had dressed carefully for this evening in a tight black skirt, short, but not too short, a black jersey top and a delicate, bright red scarf. She was too hot – but she would not remove the scarf.

Accessories made her feel more confident and sophisticated. Annoyingly, the red bangle she had worn to complement the outfit kept slipping down her arm and she had to put it in her bag.

Once again the girls moved upstairs without a win and Katie looked round to see if Al and his mates were there. They were, and Al greeted her like a long lost friend, grabbing her arm and kissing her cheek. He was wearing a distinctive aftershave that reminded Katie of mulled wine, and it seemed natural that they should sit together.

By the end of the evening all she had discovered was that he was a taxi driver. He made her laugh with stories of customers who had almost missed flights when he was on the airport run and she responded with the odd things her residents did.

It was intoxicating to be with someone who seemed to get such pleasure out of amusing her.

"What do you do other nights?" asked Al.

"I work different shifts. Some days I work earlies, most days lates, that's two until ten and then occasionally they need me to work at night, until six in the morning – but you are allowed to doze. You just have to be on call."

"And you drive yourself?"

"Yes. My husband doesn't drive." There, she'd said it, at last. She had to make certain he knew she was married. She felt a sense of relief. She had not wanted to pretend she was free. It was a pity – but she dare not encourage him. He was just too nice. She supposed he would lose interest now, but be too polite to show it.

"Don't you ever go to the theatre or the cinema?" he asked, continuing the conversation without a flicker.

"I used to – when we lived near the coast – but since I've had my daughter I just haven't thought about it."

"Do you like music? There's a show on at the pier, Songs from the Musicals. Would you like to go?"

"I'd love that – but it isn't something I'd normally…" She broke off, remembering why she had not been to any concerts or shows. Ned was uneasy in crowds and could not bear loud music.

"How about dancing? I bet you're a smashing dancer."

"I don't know. I've never really tried."

"I can't believe it. You've got natural grace. I could see when you walked in."

"Stop it. You're making me blush."

She looked round guiltily to see if anyone had noticed. Al was still talking.

"Well – how about coming to the show with me. It wouldn't have to be in the evening. It could be a matinee."

"That would be difficult. Thanks for asking, Al. I would if I could."

"Can you come with us next week?" interrupted Sally. "Jess will be back then. Her car is bigger than yours."

"Oh, I'm not sure." She looked at Al who felt for her hand and clasped it under the table. "I think I'm going somewhere else."

She felt her face burning. What was she doing? Al's hand felt so right, as if they had made a connection. Couldn't they hear her heart racing?

"Well, give us a ring if you change your mind."

No-one seemed to have noticed how flustered she was. Her mind raced through the possibilities. She would have to leave the house as usual – drive into town, park up and meet Al at the Pavilion.

"It starts at 7.30," he whispered. "I'll have the tickets. Don't worry. I'll be on my best behaviour."

"You look like a couple of conspirators," said Tania. "What's cooking?"

"Nothing," said Katie, too quickly. "Al was just telling me a joke."

"Oh yes? Why don't you share it with the rest of us?"

"Sorry, girls. Got to go. I have an extra job tonight. Be seeing you," and, with a nod to Katie, he left.

"What did you say to scare him away?" asked Sally.

"You heard him. He has to work."

Katie didn't feel like being sociable any more. She wanted to get home and hug her secret to herself. She wasn't really being wicked, was she? Didn't she deserve to enjoy herself sometimes? She wasn't planning to be unfaithful. It wasn't her fault that she and Ned didn't go anywhere together. It would certainly be more fun than Bingo, who-ever she was with. She might even tell them at home – that she was going to a show with a friend. She might – but she might not.

2

Zak arrived the following week. He wasn't staying with them. He used a hotel by the sea and drove himself up to Lane's End in a specially adapted car. The driving seat was an electric wheelchair.

Bernard was looking out for him at the gate when he pulled up. Zak pressed a lever and his chair swung round and lowered him to the roadside.

"Is it OK to leave it here, Bernard?"

"Yes, you're not blocking the stile. There's no other cars come up here. It's great to see you again."

"I came straight here. Can we look at the units later?"

"Of course. That suggestion of yours for the computer shop was just the thing."

"Have you got one yet?"

Bernard looked sheepish. "No. The one Tim had was too old fashioned."

"Well, I've had a few ideas about that. We must talk about it sometime."

They reached the back door where Rose was standing

to greet them. "Welcome, Zak. Can you come round to the front? The doors are wider there."

Bernard looked carefully at Zak's wheelchair. Of course, it would never have got over the step and through the porch. Luckily the path ran all round the house.

Zak followed Rose in through the first of the two front doors and into the dining area. "This used to be two cottages, then, Rose?"

"Yes, when they were working the chalk pit, a long time ago. My father had them knocked into one."

"Hallo, who's this?"

Heather, hearing voices, had come in from the lounge. She was pulling a fluffy dog on wheels.

"You remember Heather," said Rose. "Heather – this is Zak."

Heather stared at the wheelchair. "Why's your chair got wheels?" she asked.

"Because my legs don't work properly so it's hard for me to walk."

"I can walk – and I can run." She demonstrated by chasing round the table.

"Ah– but I can go faster in my wheelchair than I could if I was running."

"Like Jojo?" She gave the toy dog a tug. It hit the table leg and fell over.

The adults laughed.

"Yes," said Zak, "but I have to drive carefully."

"Do you want to see the chickens?"

"I'd like that. Your daddy said we could go through the orchard and down to the shop."

"Can I come too, Daddy?"

"After our cup of tea," said Rose. "Zak has come a long way to see us. Come along young lady. Help me get the cups and saucers."

Heather followed Rose into the kitchen.

"She's getting really tall. This life suits her."

"She's lovely. Sometimes I can't believe she's ours."

"How is Katie?"

At his friend's question the smile vanished from Bernard's face.

"She gets tired. She misses all the fun. Things don't feel the same, Zak. I don't know what to do."

"She might not be happy if she was here all day. At least with Rose to help you can go out together sometimes."

Bernard looked thoughtful. "She works most nights," he muttered, but he knew that was just an excuse. He'd never thought of taking his wife out in the evenings. Where would they go? He didn't know what was going on locally. She'd never suggested it. How stupid of him. All he seemed to think about was how to amuse Heather.

He thought back to the honeymoon on the canal boat, trying to visualise what made Katie happy. "I know," he said out loud, "Having a meal in a restaurant."

"Brilliant," said Zak. "That's exactly what I meant. Who would know about the best places?"

"Pat," said Rose, as she put down a tray of scones.

"Are we going to see Auntie Pat?" Heather was fidgeting in the doorway.

"Soon. Go and get one of your picture books while we finish our tea."

At the lower end of Chalk Pit Lane, instead of turning left to the main road, the trio followed the hedge bordering the campsite along Smallbridge Lane to the next turning.

"I don't think I've ever been on a road called that,

before," said Zak.

"There's a bridge over a little river along there. Heather and I play Pooh-sticks sometimes. Would you like to see?"

"How about it, Heather? Can you walk that far?"

"Yes,yes, please."

"Hold my hand, Heather," said Bernard. The road had no pavement and they let Zak lead the way. "We'll look in on Pat on the way back."

From one side of the bridge they could look up the slope of the hillside to the thick woods at the top. The water trickled down over rocks, making tiny waterfalls a few inches deep. Below the bridge it slowed. There was a deeper muddy patch in the field and then it widened as it meandered down to the sea.

They had some difficulty finding sticks but enjoyed two races before the steady clop clop of hooves heralded a group of riders. Once they had passed Bernard indicated that they ought to return.

"Pat's got ice-cream," he said as they retraced their steps.

A couple of cars were parked in the lay-by beyond the camp entrance and three more were visible by the hedge.

"You're getting busy, Bernard," commented Zak.

"Auntie Pat!" Heather ran into the shop and Pat came round the counter to hug her. "Daddy said we could have ice-cream."

Zak drove in and moved aside to let Bernard past.

"What would you like, Zak?"

"Have you an apple juice, please?"

"Pat, this is Zak, my friend from college." Pat released Heather and shook Zak's hand.

"One apple juice coming up. What for you, Bernard?"

"Two ice cream cones that you have to unwrap, Pat. The ones with the sauce on."

Heather was hopping up and down by the freezer.

"Wait a minute, child," laughed Pat. "We need a picnic table or two in the courtyard, Bernard. That bench outside isn't enough."

"Fine – as long as the vans for the computer shop can turn round."

"There's Mike now," said Pat. "It looks like he's just done a delivery."

"I'll just go over there and have a chat with him, if you don't mind," said Zak.

"Can we go and see Chantelle?" interrupted Heather.

"Yes, but not for long and don't get ice cream on anything."

Chantelle was serving a tall, thin girl in shorts when they reached the shop so they waited outside until she left.

"Hallo, Bernard, Heather. Guess what? That girl really liked my postcards. She bought ten. I'll soon have to ask Mike to print some more."

"Chantelle – can I see the clown that climbs up the pole?"

Chantelle laughed. They all watched the toy and Heather said wistfully, "I wish I had one like that."

Bernard was tempted but he knew what Katie would say, "Another five-minute wonder."

"You can see him every time you come," said Chantelle diplomatically. "How about taking a lavender bag for Nana, and one for your mum?"

"Can I have one too? What do they do?"

"They smell nice. You put them in a drawer with your clothes. Here, sniff."

Heather looked uncertain but Bernard said, "Thanks, Chantelle. Come on Heather, time we took Zak home for tea."

Heather was yawning at the table after their meal.

"She'll sleep well tonight," said Rose. "You two have a chat. I'll see to her bath."

Bernard cleared the table and sat down with his friend.

"I'm sure a computer would help you, Bernard. The keys all have capital letters."

"But I can't make words."

"You could do. Just use the letter names. It's only a smaller pattern. I've brought something to show you."

Zak took out a book with a shiny black cover. Down the side were little tags, each with a different letter of the alphabet. "It's really for telephone numbers but we can use it as a word book. You'd be surprised how many words you already know - your name for instance."

"Bernard?"

"Yes. Can you write it from memory?"

"Yes. It starts with a B."

"Good." Zak turned to the page marked B and Bernard slowly printed his name.

"Can you remember any other words that start with a B?"

"Yes, BUS and BANK."

"You write them down and see if they look right."

A slow smile spread across Bernard's face. "Now the words are in the book I'll always remember them."

"Yes, and you can find them, as long as you know the

first letter. If you can do this with all the letters you'll soon be able to use the computer."

Bernard was choked with excitement. He felt that he was at the beginning of a new journey. Just as when Eliza had taught him about mosaics, it was as if a window had been opened in his head.

Zak laughed. "It's easier than you thought, isn't it?"

"But only with you here. What can I do when you go back?"

"How about asking Chantelle? You said she was going to help you with something."

"A necklace. Can I show her the book? I'd rather ask her than Katie or Rose."

"Of course. It's yours. We can start some more letters tomorrow if I come back. How about meeting me at the shop after lunch?"

"That would be fine. Thanks, Zak."

"Don't put in words that you won't want to use just because you've seen them somewhere."

"Like car number plates. I remember those."

Zak turned his chair towards the door. "It's getting dark. I'd better get going. Say goodnight to Rose for me, and I'll see you tomorrow."

Bernard felt tired, tired of concentrating and afraid he might disappoint his friend. He smiled weakly and followed him to his car. He wished he didn't have such vivid memories of his first school. Bigger than the other children, he had always been expected to do more, but all the sounds had blurred together in his head and he was constantly writing the little letters back to front.

He had been christened James, after his father, and Bernard after Anne's grandfather. The teacher let him put JIM on his pictures until he had taken one home to his father and saw it ripped up before his eyes.

"If you can't write James at your age, be Bernard the Booby – that's what you are."

He was seven when his father left. He and his mother never heard from him again. After a short stay in a special school she took him home and spent her time reading and re-reading all her favourite stories. No-one seemed to expect much of him and he was content not having to read or write.

It was not until he was in his thirties and had to fend for himself after her death that he had discovered he could make a living for himself from his natural creativity.

From building mosaics to gardening, he developed skills that gave him the opportunity to work and support his family.

He knew it was his artistic talent that had first endeared him to Katie – that, and his gentle manner. Now he was a market gardener she didn't treat him quite the same. They had lost something since they moved to Lane's End. He wished he knew how to get it back.

His mind turned to the present he wanted to create. When the old woman in the houseboat had wanted to design a mosaic she had looked in books for illustrations to copy. That's what he'd do. He'd look for magazines with pictures of models and celebrities and see what their jewellery was like.

Now he had some watering to do. The currant bushes had been planted near the house, away from the camp site in case they were too tempting for the visitors.

He'd do that before he went in.

The nearer Friday came the more guilty Katie felt.

Her mood swung from defiant to excited. One minute she was fussing round Ned and Heather as if she was making up for the time she was intending to spend not thinking about them – the next she was trying to avoid her mother's eye. Did Rose sense something had changed in her daughter?

It was a relief to be at work at Evergreens, making sure the elderly residents were happy and competent. It was Thursday afternoon when she realised why she didn't enjoy the Bingo. Every month the residents gathered in the lounge for a game. Instead of cash the prizes were boxes of biscuits or pot plants but it still felt like entertainment for old people. They would be really surprised if they could see the swish setting with all the lights and buttons that she had discovered in the Bingo Hall.

By Friday evening she had convinced herself that this was definitely a one-off. She would leave as if she was going to Bingo, but never again would she make a date with a man who was not her husband. However – she had done it and she intended to enjoy it.

She parked the car in a side street some way from the pier. She'd walk along the prom and settle her nerves. If only they'd asked two of the others and gone in a group – but she didn't dare not turn up. The only number she had for Al was the taxi company.

She saw him, then, leaning on the railings of the pier – staring out to sea. He looked smaller than she remembered, only a little taller than she was, but then he turned and the generous mouth flashed a smile. "You're early."

Just hearing his voice made her tingle with excitement. She tried to sound calm as she replied, "Yes. I didn't want to pay for parking. You looked lost in thought."

"I was just enjoying the view. No seaweed smell tonight. The wind must be in another direction." They laughed together and she began to relax.

"Do you want a drink or anything before it starts?"

"No thanks, but get one if you want."

"I could order coffee for the interval – or we could opt for an ice-cream. It can get hot in there."

"I think that would be better." As they walked slowly up the steps to the theatre his hand found hers. It made her feel childlike and safe.

Kate remembered the last time she had been here. She had been pregnant with Heather and had made sure Ned had a seat by the aisle. It had been a pantomime – one she felt he would enjoy. Aladdin had been the perfect choice for someone who loved colour and jewels. The music had not been too loud and the experience had been more successful than she had hoped. But Heather was three now and they had never gone again.

"I wonder what the pantomime will be this year," she said out loud.

"Why? Would you like to go?"

"I might take Heather. She's just about old enough to sit through it."

"Well, let's get seated now. I think the show's starting soon."

If she could have relaxed, singing along with all the tunes she knew, forgetting herself in the shared experience, she might have enjoyed the evening. As it was, she hardly heard the music – she was too hot, too aware of a strange man beside her, too riven with guilt and too nervous about what might happen next.

By the time they left the hall she wasn't even sure she was fit to drive home.

"I'll see you to your car." Al seemed as chirpy as ever as he linked arms and set off along the prom.

Katie was suddenly afraid someone who knew her might see them. She pretended to scrabble in her bag for a tissue and then put her hands in her pockets and sped up. He was too close, as if he felt they belonged together.

"What's up, babe?"

"Don't call me that. I'm just a bit cold, that's all. I think this might have been a mistake."

"You didn't enjoy it?"

"I'm sorry, Al. It felt a bit…strange. I would have felt better in a group."

"I thought as much. It was my fault. I just thought it was your sort of thing."

"It was – but next time let's make it a group outing, shall we?"

Al beamed with pleasure. "You'll come out again?"

"I'd like to, if Cam and Tania come too."

"I've got the very thing. It would have to be on a Monday. We all go to a quiz night at the White Hart. It's near the wildlife centre. Do you know it?"

"That's where mum used to take me to feed the ducks."

"Well, the pub's a bit further along that road. They're a great crowd. It would do you good."

"Maybe. I'll tell you Friday. Here's my car," She ducked away from his kiss and, unlocking the door, slid behind the wheel.

She hardly saw his wave as she sped away from the kerb – her heart beating as if she had just escaped from a dangerous situation.

She felt confused, relieved, excited and 'young,' – as if, too late, she was experiencing the joys of dating. Had she been a fool to marry the first man who showed her any affection – or was she being foolish now? Was she risking losing all that had made her content?

She slowed down and tried to concentrate on her driving. She needed to get home and think about what to do next.

It was Sunday before Bernard plucked up courage enough to ask Katie if she would like to go for a meal. He'd told Pat what he intended to do and she had suggested they try the King's Head now it had been turned into a gastro-pub.

He couldn't understand why it felt so awkward, just talking to his wife, but he hadn't wanted to ask her while Heather or Rose were about, so he waited until they were alone in their bedroom.

"Would you like to go out for a meal, sometime?" he blurted out.

"What did you say?"

"We could go out to dinner – like we used to – if Rose wouldn't mind." The more he said, the more he felt she would say no.

"I don't know, Ned. I'm not around much in the evenings, am I? Let me think about it. This is a real surprise. When did you want to go?"

"I hadn't thought. I just felt it might be nice."

He wished he hadn't said anything. She didn't look pleased, just puzzled.

"How about I tell you in the morning?"

She climbed into bed and lay looking at the ceiling.

Bernard got in beside her. He didn't know whether to touch her or not. It had been so easy when they were first married. Why couldn't they understand each other any more?

Katie gave him a swift peck on the cheek and turned over, away from him.

Would he ever know what she was thinking again? he wondered.

Next morning Katie woke early and came back from the bathroom with a big smile on her face.

"I've got the answer," she said, before Bernard was properly awake.

"We'll go for lunch – not dinner. We can have it at the café on the pier. That would be a real treat – being able to see the sea while we had our meal. Then I could go on to work and you could do whatever you liked. There are some new shops you might like to look at. How does that sound?"

Bernard blinked. He hadn't even had time to suggest the King's Head. She seemed to have worked it all out while he was asleep. It wasn't quite what he'd intended but if it would make her happy that's all that mattered – and they would be alone together, without Rose and Heather.

Katie sounded enthusiastic. "How about Thursday?" she said.

"Yes. That would be nice," he responded, feeling that, as usual, the decisions had all been made before he'd had time to consider them.

On Wednesday morning at the playgroup Katie was wondering what to tell the girls about her date. Would Al let the cat out of the bag? Should she be honest – or would they tease her or, worse still, condemn her?

She was saved by Tania who greeted her with the words, "Cam says you're coming to the quiz on Monday."

"I might be," Katie stuttered.

"Al told him he'd seen you going into the show with a friend. Was it someone from work?"

"Yes," she lied. "They had a spare ticket."

"I said I'm surprised he let you go in without him."

"What did he say?"

"That it wasn't his sort of thing. He's a Queen fan."

"Who's a Queen fan?" asked Sally as she joined them.

"Al," said Tania. "He's got Katie to come to the pub with us next week."

"I didn't say next week." She was feeling pressured, although she was down for an early shift on Monday.

"Well – Cam's picking me up at seven thirty. If you like we'll take you too."

It really did seem too good an opportunity to miss. Rose and Ned would see Cam and Tania and know she was going in a group. She would be able to tell them about it afterwards and not keep secrets.

"I'm not very good at general knowledge," she said.

"It's all done in a team. You'd be surprised what you find you know."

"I want a drink, Mummy," It was Oliver, astride a plastic engine.

"OK. I'll get you some orange."

Katie turned to Sally. "What happens to Oliver when she keeps going out?"

"Jess takes him. He loves playing with her boy. He often stays overnight."

Katie looked round for Heather. She was digging clothes out of a dressing up box and wrapping herself in a large piece of net.

"Look, Mummy, I'm a princess."

Katie laughed. Heather's honey-blonde hair was

getting long. She was tall for three and uncannily like the image of Alice in the Lewis Carroll books.

Alice! That name could solve one problem she had been concerned about. She was not a good liar and had been afraid Al's name would come out in conversation at home – but if she thought of him as Alice it would not matter. She would definitely go on Monday.

Ned would understand. It was not his sort of thing. She'd make it up to him somehow. Happily she delved into the box and pulled out an embroidered velvet waistcoat.

"Here, Heather. This would look nice."

It was a relief to concentrate on her daughter rather than constantly comparing the two men in her life.

3

While Katie was at playgroup, Bernard approached Chantelle again.

She told him she would be glad to help but he felt awkward going to her on his own, especially at her place of work. It had been different learning how to make Katie's necklace. If anyone came in he looked as if he belonged there – but he couldn't stand the thought of a stranger catching him learning words.

Chantelle had the answer.

"What we need is LEXICON."

"What's that?"

"It's one of the games I sell. It's a card game – all in capitals. I'll show you."

She picked a small box from the shelf and took out the cards, spreading them across the counter. Choosing carefully, she made three words: IS IT IN.

"Can you see the difference?"

"Yes." Bernard was beaming now. "They all start the same but end with a different letter."

"Can you hear the difference?"

"Say them again."

She did – and Bernard pointed to each one as she did so.

"Now you do it."

"IS IT IN – it sounds like a question."

"That's why I chose them. You only have to add two words and you've got a sentence."

"Chantelle, that's so clever."

"And, if anyone comes in I'm showing you the game. I'd better get some more in stock. I'll put these away now until we've finished the necklace."

Bernard watched her get out the three strands of semi-precious stones, connected by a web of tiny beads, glittering green, red and amber. All it needed was a clasp.

"When are you going to give it to her?"

"I don't know. We don't go anywhere special."

"I thought you were going to take her for a meal?"

"I was – but she said it would be better if we went at lunchtime. We're going tomorrow, to that nice café by the beach. She said she could then drive on to work and I could have a look at the shops before I came home."

"Did you want to do that?"

"Well, it's a long time since I saw the sea. I'd rather go swimming."

"Why don't you take your trunks and a towel and do what you want. Can you get back by yourself?"

"Oh,yes. I'll get the bus." The idea of going swimming again made him feel better. He was nervous about having the meal alone with Katie.

It had been over a year since they had done anything like that. Could he give her the necklace then? He wanted so much to show her he still loved her.

It was fine the next day. Bernard dressed carefully and put the box containing the necklace in the base of his backpack with a towel and shorts on top. He had not told Katie he was going swimming. It seemed wrong, somehow, to be taking the afternoon off while she was working.

There were a few people eating outside the café but most of the tables inside were free.

"The ploughman's looks reasonable," suggested Katie. "If we have to spend all that money on parking we don't want anything expensive. What shall we have with it, tea?"

"Yes, please."

"You find a table near the window. I'll order." Bernard found a place and waited for Katie to join him.

"Now, what made you think of doing this?" To his relief she was smiling.

"I was talking to Zak," he said, "I told him we didn't do much." He lifted his bag onto his lap.

Katie watched, her smile fading.

"I've made you something." He was digging in his bag for the box.

"What on earth have you got there?"

"Just a towel. Never mind that. This is for you. I made it." He placed the box before her on the table.

Katie wiped her hands on her skirt and carefully opened the box. Her face flushed crimson as she lifted the necklace from its nest of tissue paper.

"Ned. You made this? For me? I don't deserve it."

"Yes you do. Chantelle taught me how to do it. Do you like it?"

"It's absolutely beautiful and the colours are my favourites. Thank you, Ned. I don't know what to say."

Their attention was diverted by the arrival of their meals.

Bernard was delighted. Katie was animated and attentive, asking him questions and waiting for the answers, just as she used to do.

They were finishing with coffee when she asked, "How are you going to stop people stealing the apples?"

"I'm going to go out at night. Most campers are couples but some families have children who might be able to climb the new wall round the car park or get in through the hedge. Rose says she'd like another dog."

Katie pushed away her cup. "I know what Mum says, and what Chantelle says and what Zak says. Don't you ever have a single thought that's your own?"

Bernard was shocked by the accusation and his face must have registered his dismay because Katie apologised immediately.

"I'm sorry, Ned. That was unfair. I'm tired. I think I need a break."

Bernard seized on the suggestion. "Do you think we could have a holiday?"

"You mean go away somewhere with Heather? It would have to be after the harvest. We'll see. I'd better get a move on, now. That was a beautiful present, Ned. I'll take it in the car, shall I? I'm sorry I snapped at you."

He followed her meekly out of the café. With the box in the boot of the car she gave him a swift kiss and drove away.

Had the meal been the success he had hoped? It had almost been perfect but there still hadn't seemed enough time. He wasn't sure he felt like swimming now.

He walked along the promenade past the pier and towards the swimming pool. It was when he heard children laughing that he realised he was passing the adventure playground. It had cages full of coloured balls, high plastic slides, a funny house on stilts, a little train and a sandpit. Heather would love this, he thought. They must bring her here soon.

Pleased to have made a decision he turned towards the beach, undressed quickly next to a groyne and hobbled over the pebbles to the sea.

He'd forgotten how cold it was when you first went in – but once his whole body was submerged he struck out strongly. When he was well away from the beach he turned over onto his back and floated, his body rising and falling with the waves. The buildings along the front gleamed in the afternoon sun. He'd missed this. He'd been so busy with the smallholding and the campsite and Heather that he'd forgotten what it was like to have fun, to feel free.

Towelling himself down, he felt invigorated, refreshed and ready for anything.

It didn't even bother him that it was the first time he had travelled alone on the bus. He arrived back at Lane's End feeling as if he had conquered the world, or, at least, many of his own fears.

Heather ran to meet him. "Look, Daddy. Look what I've found." The tiny green caterpillar was arching across a leaf.

"That's pretty," he said, wondering where she had found it. He had a feeling it was a pest on fruit trees. He needed to check the orchard.

"It's all right, Bernard," said Rose as they entered the kitchen. "She found it in the hedge. I think the trees are safe."

"I'm sorry. I should have been here."

"Don't be silly. Did you have a nice time?"

"Yes. I really did. Katie loved the necklace and I found somewhere else we could go. I'll tell you later."

"What happened to your hair?"

"I went in the sea. It was wonderful."

"Can I go in the sea, Daddy? I want to go in the sea."

"It was very cold, darling but we'll go down when mummy has a day off. I promise."

He saw Rose beaming at them both and felt happy for the first time in months.

"You look nice," said Bernard as Katie came downstairs after tea on Monday night.

"It's because I've got heels on. Actually I'm a bit nervous. I hope they don't expect me to be clever."

"You aren't taking the car?" said Rose.

"No. Tania is picking me up."

"Is Sally going?"

"Not this week. The family are away in the South of France, I think."

"Will you be back late?"

"I don't know. I don't know when it finishes. I'll call you if it's going to be a problem."

Katie really was nervous – and not only because it was a quiz.

When they had gone upstairs after their Bingo games on Friday she had finally won a line and was eager to tell Al, but he hadn't been there.

"He says he'll see you on Monday at the White Hart," Cameron told her. "He had a long distance job on tonight. He couldn't turn it down."

The evening had been ruined for Katie. She missed Al's lively chatter, the stories and the compliments. She hadn't realised how much she looked forward to just seeing him smile at her.

She'd wanted to ask him about the kind of questions they had in the quiz. Should she read up on politics or watch different television programmes? There wasn't time – all she could do was hope she didn't make a fool of herself.

There was a toot from the lane. Cameron and Tania had arrived.

"I'll see you in the morning, Heather," she called out as she shut the porch door and hurried down the path.

By the end of the evening Katie had the beginnings of a headache. Al had been pleased to see her but, in company, tended to be the joker in the pack. Everyone else seemed to be so relaxed and it was difficult when the only people she recognised were Tania and Cameron.

It wasn't until questions on health and nature came up that she felt brave enough to make suggestions. She hadn't realised how specialised the medical knowledge she had gained at work was.

Al was impressed. "How do you know so much about bones, eyes and ears?" he said.

"I have to. I have to know what's wrong with the people in my care. They can't always tell you. I've just picked it up over the years. You were brilliant on the music round."

"Yes, but we only came third. If Maurice had been here we would have won. He's better than me on Geography."

"We'll have you on our team again," Cameron said to Katie. "What would you like to drink?"

"Another white wine, please."

"You look terrific," said Al once they had been served and the conversation had turned to the progress of the local football team. "Can I drive you home?"

"Oh. I came with Cameron."

"They may be very late. I've got the taxi. It will just look as if you got a cab back."

Katie was thrilled at the suggestion. It would be wonderful not to be the driver for a change and being alone in the car with Al would feel dangerously intimate. As she accepted and followed him out of the pub her subconscious told her she was playing with fire but she damped it down. After all, Al had always been the perfect gentleman. He wouldn't risk that by compromising her, would he?

"Along the Front or over the Downs?" asked Al as they set off.

"Over the Downs, please." There was less likelihood of someone seeing them if they went home that way.

"Could you be a regular team member?" asked Al.

"Not if I have every Friday night off for Bingo."

"Which would you rather go to?"

"The quiz. It was fun. I'll see if I can change shifts permanently. I don't think the girls would miss me now they don't need me to drive them."

"You really do know things the others don't know. It was great having you there."

Al slowed the car and parked in a lay-by.

"What's up?" Her voice was a strange croak. Something had happened to her breathing.

"Nothing. I hoped you'd give me a goodnight kiss and it seemed a better place to stop than outside your house."

Katie hesitated. Last time they'd kissed it hadn't seemed a big deal. Did she owe him that for including her tonight? Before she could answer her own question

Al had unclasped his seat belt and turned towards her, kissing her full on the mouth.

Whether it was because she'd been drinking, or the touch of his fingers on her neck, or the fact that she was still confined – she didn't know – but her body responded to his kiss. Her back arched, her legs parted and her insides felt on fire. She rode the wave of feeling with an intensity she had never experienced before, but as Al turned his head, the sweet, sickly smell of mulled wine brought her to her senses. This should not be happening!

She struggled to push him off. "Don't."

"I knew you had it in you." His voice was triumphant. "When did you last feel like that?"

He shouldn't have spoken. It made her think of Ned and her sense of excitement turned immediately to shame. She burst into tears.

Al pulled away – his face registering concern.

"I'm sorry, Katie – don't cry. I didn't mean to upset you."

Katie felt in her bag for a tissue. "Can we go now?" she said, shakily.

All she could think about was getting home. How had this happened? Why was her body so out of control? What was it about this man that made her feel so different?

"Yes, of course," Al said miserably.

The rest of the journey was completed in silence. At the end of Chalk Pit Lane he placed his hand gently on her arm.

"I really like being with you. Forgive me?"

"I can't think now. Are my eyes red?"

"No, you look fine."

"Goodnight, Al." She left the car without a backward glance. Her legs felt wobbly as she tried to walk up the path to the back door. She hoped she looked steadier than she felt. It was a relief to get indoors and collapse on the nearest seat.

Her insides were still churning – but no longer with passion. She tried to analyse how she felt – thrilled, sad, angry, afraid – all those things. She was thrilled that she could feel like that, sad that it was with another man, angry at herself for getting into the situation and afraid that she might be found out – or that she might want it to happen again.

She put the kettle on for a cup of tea. Whatever else had happened she'd had a shock and she needed to settle her nerves before she went up to bed.

Rose found it difficult to put into words how grateful she felt that Bernard and Katie had come to live with her.

She was acutely aware that it wasn't by choice – that it had been forced on them by circumstances and that there had really been no need for Heather to have been considered for adoption. Bernard had been more than capable of looking after his daughter and although the houseboat was not an ideal home it may have been only temporary.

Bernard's horticulture course had qualified him for work in nurseries or gardens but it had also given him the skills needed to cultivate the land at Lane's End. Without him she would have had to employ someone or sell up.

Now she was determined to reward him and was busy at her sewing machine when Bernard came in from the kitchen.

"That looks pretty," he said, "What is it?"

"New curtains. I thought it was about time we used

Tim's office. I've chosen some paint and a new carpet. I don't want to call it The Office any more. How about, The Study?"

"What will we use it for?"

"I've been watching you since Zak left. You are studying, aren't you? Is Chantelle helping you?"

"Yes." Bernard blushed. "We are collecting words. Zak says when I know enough he'll show me how to use a computer."

"That's what I thought. It would have to be somewhere quiet – away from the television. We need a study."

"Will it be green and yellow?"

"Yes. I hope you like it." She held up the curtains. "I thought buttercup yellow for the walls and emerald green for the carpet. That would be a change from the cream and brown in there now."

She'd hardly been in the room since the police took away her husband's belongings. The black desk and cubed shelving were still there. At first she had thought of it as a potential playroom for Heather, until she realised that meant shutting her away from everyone else. Now Bernard could use it for his writing and she could sort out the business in peace. They had an accountant but keeping track of finances for the smallholding, the units and the campsite was quite time-consuming and produced a great deal of paper.

Perhaps if Zak got Bernard a computer she could learn how to use it. She must try not to be afraid of new inventions. Heather would be growing into a world where computers were commonplace and Rose didn't want to be left behind.

"Will you be happy working in a yellow room, Bernard? It could be green if you preferred?"

"No. I think yellow is fine. It's a happy colour. Thank you, Rose. You have such good ideas."

"Daddy, look at me?"

Heather came in from the lounge. She was draped in the old curtains from the office, thick burgundy velour. She tugged at the material as it dragged along the floor.

"Hold on, darling. You look like a queen – but you need a crown. Let's go and make one. I'll hold your train and we'll see if there is any cardboard in the kitchen."

Rose smiled as she heard them empty a cereal box and collect scissors and tape. They would be happy for a while, playing together. Heather was so lucky. How many other children had a father who was home all day and who could find time to play with them?

Towards the end of July things were always busy for Rose. Most of the soft fruit had been picked and the apples were ripening in the orchard.

It would not be long before they would need every moment to pick the apples. Tim and his brother used to do it without help and Rose wondered if George would take a few days off to assist them this year.

The young couple had suggested they might like to take Heather away for a holiday. That would be a good idea. The atmosphere between them had been strained for weeks. Each seemed absorbed in their own worlds. Katie was due a holiday and it would do Bernard good to get away from Lane's End for a while.

Rose had taken a stall at the Sheep Fair and sold jam, pies and cakes. Being there reminded her of the times she had watched her husband and his dog competing. Poor Jenny had lasted 16 years but was blind by the time she died last November.

Rose had wanted to get another dog straight away but Katie insisted that they wait until Heather was older. Now she was looking forward to the apple harvest and collecting jars for the chutney.

The phone in the kitchen rang and she picked it up. The voice at the other end was breathless and urgent.

"Rose, there's been an accident by the bridge. We've phoned for an ambulance but my horse has bolted. It's heading your way. Can you round up some people from the village. I'm afraid he'll hurt himself."

"Sheila. What happened?"

"A motorbike. They didn't see us as we came over the bridge. There's someone in the water. I must go. You know my mobile number."

"Yes, of course. Which horse is it?"

"Duke, the chestnut."

"Right. I'll ring the vet and the pub. We'll find him."

"He was heading for the trees. Thanks, Rose."

She put the phone down and called out, "Can you give me a hand, please, Bernard?"

He came at once.

"Do you know Sheila's horse, Duke?"

"I think so."

"Well – he's got loose and she's asked me to help find him. I'm going to ring the village but you could go out straight away. He's gone into the woods on the other side of Stable Lane. Take your phone and a rope. I'll stay here with Heather. If you find him bring him back here."

She didn't tell him about the collision. She hoped that was all under control.

Bernard was not to stay ignorant for long. As he came out of the orchard and crossed the road a motorbike pulled up next to him. It was a girl – one Bernard knew.

"Bernard, wait – I'm coming too."

"Rachel! Did you see what happened?"

"Not exactly. When I got there Rod was in the water with the bike on his legs. It wasn't very deep – but he couldn't move. I couldn't watch, Bernard. It was too much. I stayed while the ambulance came. He was moaning. The boys were arguing about whether they should move anything."

"Rose never told me it was an accident. He wasn't drowning?"

"No. The paramedics took charge. They let the others shift the bike and put Rod on a stretcher and took him to hospital. Some followed the ambulance. Others went back to Pat's. I couldn't, Bernard. It reminded me of Craig - so I thought I'd help find the horse."

"Rose said he'd gone up here. He's not in the field. Let's try the woods."

Rachel left her bike by the gate and they followed the hedge line to the top corner and climbed over a stile and into the trees.

"Why would he go up here?" she wondered out loud.

"He's scared. I don't think he knew where he was going. Perhaps he's hurt."

"Where does this path go?"

"Over the hill behind the village and then down to another road. After that it's just fields. We'd be able to see him then."

The path met a bridleway and the pair had to choose which way to turn.

"I think that way goes down to the river," said Bernard.

"Let's go up," said Rachel. "The higher we are, the more we'll be able to see. Wait! Can you hear something?"

They were silent for a while but all they heard was the wind.

"I thought it sounded like breathing," said Rachel. "Do you like horses?"

"Goodness, no. I don't know anything about them. I just wanted to do something useful."

"I can't ride one. If we find him we'll have to walk him home."

They forged on to the top of the rise and came out into the open. The view beneath them was breathtakingly beautiful-the curve of the land, divided into large fields of green and brown by neat hedgerows – the row of poplars on the distant skyline and the narrow lane snaking across the landscape.

They could see cars parked at the roadside and people getting out.

"It must be the villagers," said Bernard.

A tiny figure was waving his arms and the people were dividing up into small groups. Rachel looked round. "What do we do now? Two of them are coming up here."

"Let's go back – take the other path. I can't see him here, can you?"

Something made them both turn and run. What had seemed like an adventure had developed into a competition. Bernard felt that he'd been asked to find the horse and he wanted to be the first to see it.

In fact, he was the second. It was Rachel who spotted the chestnut as it stood, shivering, by the river, half hidden by a clump of bushes.

She grabbed Bernard's hand. "Shh, Bernard, look."

The horse hadn't seen them. Its sides were flecked

with foam and, as they watched, it jerked its head and then shook its mane.

"I think he's caught," whispered Rachel. "We can't just go hurtling down there. We'll have to take him by surprise."

"If we follow the hedge to that clump of trees we'll be hidden until we reach him."

"Perhaps we should split up – but there's no cover the other way. No, we'll stick together. You be ready with the rope. I'll try to grab the bridle."

"Don't get behind him. They kick."

"I'd kick if I was scared. Come on."

"I wish we had sugar lumps or a carrot."

"I've got some mints. Do they like mints?"

"It's worth a try."

Bernard let Rachel lead the way and watched as she took a mint out of the packet and held it ready to offer the horse. They paused in the bushes for a moment but the animal whinnied and they guessed he sensed they were there.

Rachel stepped forward murmuring soothingly, "There, Duke, don't be scared. Look at what I've got for you." Her eyes on the horse's face, she held out one hand with the mint and groped for the bridle with the other.

The horse backed away but did not rear up as Bernard had feared. He could see the trapped bridle and took hold further up, near the horse's neck. At the sight of him the horse pulled away and stamped but Rachel spoke again – tempting him with the sweet. Leaving Bernard to control the horse she reached up and stroked Duke's nose with her free hand. Then she stood back as Bernard lassoed the horse who shook and bucked but could not get free.

Once the bridle was untangled from the bush they

could steady the still shivering horse.

"His front legs are all scratched," said Rachel. "Poor thing, do you think he wants a drink?"

"I think he needs a blanket. Let's go back."

Bernard gave a gentle tug on the rope and, with Rachel walking on the other side holding the bridle and feeding him mints, they coaxed the horse up the hill.

"At least he hasn't broken anything," said Rachel.

"He likes you."

"He likes mints."

There were voices in the woods when they reached the junction and two men came walking briskly towards them.

"You've got him," said one.

"Yes," said Rachel. "He was down by the river."

"Hallo, old thing," the other man walked up to Duke and patted his neck. "You are in a state, aren't you?" He ran his hand down each leg and nodded.

"He's OK. We'll take him, now, thanks. We've got a horsebox on the road."

"And you are?" grunted Rachel.

"Nathan Brown – I'm a vet. I have treated Duke. Sheila knows me."

"So, Mr Brown. You take him."

Reluctantly Bernard passed the rope to the vet. "That belongs to Rose," he said.

"Fine. Well done, you two. It's Bernard, isn't it?"

"Yes."

"We'll let you know how he gets on," and they turned away leading the subdued horse along the track.

"Now I suppose we'd better find out what happened to Rod," said Rachel. "Pat will give us a cup of tea. Come on."

51

Bernard was relieved. He wanted to talk to Chantelle. Katie had been so strange lately. He hoped she would be proud of him when he told her what he had done today.

The motorcyclists were gathered outside Pat's shop.

"Visiting hours are until 8 o'clock," said one when Rachel asked about Rod. "Penny and Greg are there. The docs say he should be able to come out in a few days. No broken bones-he was just shocked and bruised."

"The bike was on top of him."

"Yes – but the bed of the river was so uneven and his leathers so tough he didn't take all the weight. He was lucky."

"The bike's not so lucky," said another voice. "The forks are bent and it was full of water. The electrics are shot."

"We can sort that out. Let's get some chow. Coming, Rachel?"

"Yes – if that's all right with you, Bernard?"

"I've got to see someone. Thanks for all your help. You tell them." Of course their friend was more important than a horse but he'd enjoy telling Chantelle about their afternoon. She was a great listener.

4

Katie had made up her mind. There would be no repetition of Monday night. She would ensure she was never alone in a vehicle with Al again. She would not go to the quiz. She would keep her shifts as they were. It was convenient for her to work Friday mornings and be home all day Saturday. She would still go to the Bingo and if she saw Al there he'd just be one of the crowd. She could manage that.

Her head told her it was all settled. She refused to listen to the voice inside her that warned her she was making a mistake – that there was no way she could pretend that she had felt nothing when Al kissed her and that, once roused, those feelings were unlikely to go away.

She would not admit to herself that she did not want to give up seeing him completely – that he had become a drug that she depended on to make her life enjoyable and that nothing else had given her the feeling of power that knowing he desired her had done.

She roused her daughter, dressed her, gave her

breakfast and went to see to the chickens. Together, they watched Ned, as he built the new wall that Katie had requested between the lawn and the vegetable garden.

Once the private area between the house and the woods was made separate she might stop feeling that their whole lives were public property. It was bad enough when Rose had had guests in the house but now the campsite was in the bottom field Katie felt as if the whole homestead was open to invasion. After all, what was there between the campers and the house? Two hedges and one gate. Even the greenhouse with the tomatoes was only just in view from the kitchen.

She loved the little cherry tomatoes that were ripening fast. It was good being able to eat fruit and vegetables they had grown themselves but they didn't have enough land to be commercial. Living here would always be a struggle. She had hoped marriage would be her passport out of such responsibilities – away from somewhere that was so much her father's domain – but she felt trapped, caged, like a hamster, as if she were destined to run forever in the same endless wheel.

Still, she could at least fashion her surroundings to her taste, and watching Ned place the grey-pink textured blocks carefully on top of one another she was struck by how he brought out feelings of tenderness in her that even her daughter did not evoke. It was the feeling one had when the underdog wins the race, a mixture of pride, joy and relief.

"You're making a lovely job of that, Ned," she said and was rewarded with a large grin. Ned seemed so much more confident and contented since the incident with the horse. If only they could do something exciting together.

Her throat felt dry and her voice had come out

as a croak. She hoped she wasn't coming down with something.

A lot of the staff with school age children were on holiday and she was needed at work to supervise the young ones, many of whom did not speak much English. She would dose herself up over the weekend. They would have to go out as a family another time.

George was back for the weekend and Rose had invited him and Pat to lunch on Sunday. It should have been an enjoyable family occasion but Katie had been in bed for two days with a severe cough and a temperature. Bernard had moved into Heather's room and his daughter was sleeping on a camp bed in the master bedroom.

"She's had a little Bovril," said Rose as she sat down at the table where Bernard was carving the joint.

"She's better off resting," said Pat. "I'll go and see her later."

"This looks terrific, Rose," said George, piling vegetables onto his plate. "I don't know anyone who can cook like you."

"And no-one can talk and eat like you do," chivvied Pat.

George had been telling them about the characters he had met on his drive up the M1. "There was this fellow in Carlisle who was moaning that he had a two bedroom flat just south of Blackpool that he rented out for holidays and a family had just cancelled. I thought it would be great if you and I could have a week there, Pat. What do you think?"

"When is it vacant?"

"In a couple of weeks."

"In September? Don't be daft. The shop will be busy then – the site is booked up until late October. Besides, if I'm to have a holiday I don't want to go self-catering. I was planning on a Turkey and Tinsel weekend in a nice hotel, you skinflint!"

"Is it by the sea?" asked Bernard.

"Yes. Are you interested?"

"I think so. How much would it cost?"

"Not much. Getting there will cost more. I've got his number. Talk to Katie. Could you get away then?"

Bernard looked at Rose. "Will we be finished by then?"

"That's what I was going to ask you about, George," she said, "Could you take a week off to help with the apples?"

"Well – if we aren't going away, sure. I need a break. They look nearly ready."

"We've already had some. If the weather's good the main crop should be perfect in the next two weeks. The others could wait until Bernard came back."

"Are we going to the seaside, Daddy?" piped up Heather.

"If Mummy is better. We have to keep giving her the medicine and letting her sleep so that she can get well again."

"Can I get down, now?"

"Hold on, poppet. What about pudding?" said Pat.

"There's apple pie and ice-cream," said Rose.

"I only want ice-cream."

"There's one person that doesn't care about the apples," Pat chuckled.

Bernard was excited. He wanted to get out a map and find

out where Blackpool was. He wished Katie had been with them and suspected she would not share his enthusiasm. How could he make her see that this was the chance they had been waiting for?

He was piling up the plates for Rose when his mother-in-law said, "Don't worry, Bernard. I'll get her to think it was her idea. Leave it to me. Why don't you take some chairs out on the lawn?"

"Can I show Auntie Pat my garden?" asked Heather.

"Yes, of course. Let's all get some sun." George led the way through the front door and looked up at the woods. "This is some slope, Bernard, but the grass looks great and you've made a fine job of that wall."

The two men went round the side of the house to the porch for the seats while Heather dragged Pat towards the patch of ground they had planted with pansies.

"Look, Auntie Pat. The flowers have faces."

"I can see. Can you tell me the colours?"

"Yes. That one's yellow, that one's purple and that one's white, mostly."

George and Bernard came back with four garden chairs.

"It seems funny without a dog," said George once they had sat down.

"That's what Rose thinks – she's going to ask Katie again"

"Will she agree?"

"I hope so." Bernard sighed. "I don't like her being ill."

"It's nothing serious. She just needs a holiday."

Katie came out of the bathroom and paused when she heard voices in the garden. It wasn't fair that she should be excluded from such a jolly family occasion. She tried to speak but her voice was a painful croak and she wandered back into the bedroom and turned her pillow over to get the cool side. One moment she was boiling hot and the next she was shivering. She sat up until a fit of coughing had subsided and then lay down – her hair sticking to her forehead with sweat.

She couldn't remember ever feeling so ill – but the doctor had given her some antibiotics and said all she needed was a good rest.

Sally had phoned to ask how she was and offered to take Heather to playgroup. It irritated her that they could manage without her, but then everything irritated her at present. She didn't dare look at herself in the mirror. She knew she'd see a red-nosed, blotchy-faced harridan.

Life was such a muddle. She couldn't seem to enjoy anything. Yet it felt like her own fault. Perhaps it was because she was ill. She'd go back to sleep and hope things would seem easier when she woke up.

Once the holiday was booked, there was little Katie could do about it. Rose had done as she had promised, mentioned George's plan and Pat's refusal and left Katie to come to the same conclusion as her husband. By the time she was better, George had paid the small deposit that was all his contact had requested and Rose had paid for the train tickets in advance.

This would be her last free Friday evening before they were due to go away. Katie couldn't go out the night before their trip – it would seem too selfish and, besides, she couldn't leave all the packing and preparation to Ned.

She surveyed herself in the bedroom mirror. Her hair

was getting long. She had washed it and it curled over her shoulders. Her trousers were chocolate brown and quite close fitting. Her shirt was silky gold and over it she wore a mock-leather jacket. She'd bought a new pair of boots, claiming she needed them for the holiday – but they were more fashionable than practical. She felt in command, looking good but unavailable. She would show Al she enjoyed his company but she was not ready for it to develop into a relationship.

She drove herself down to the Bingo. She wanted to relish her new independence.

The hall seemed stuffy after the fresh night air. Katie had forgotten how bright the lighting was and longed for the games to be completed so they could join the men upstairs. Would Al be there? It was such a long time since she'd seen him. Perhaps he'd found someone else. She was aware of her face reddening as she entered the bar and her heart gave a leap as she saw him talking with Cameron and Blogger.

He turned towards her and his smile made her weak with relief. He held out both arms and clasped her hands in his. "I heard you'd been ill. Are you OK now?"

She gripped him eagerly, trying to convey so much with the pressure of her fingers – joy, familiarity- but most of all gratitude, gratitude that he still cared about her in spite of her behaviour. She wasn't close enough – she let go his hands and flung herself into his embrace, hugging him and laughing, all her good intentions flown.

Gently he steered her towards a bench. "You sit down – I'll get your drink. What will it be?"

"Could I have a Martini?" she giggled.

"Red? With lemonade?"

"Yes. I suppose so."

"What's this - a night for experimenting?"

"Maybe." Was she flirting? If so, it felt like fun.

"Where are Sally and Jess?" Al asked as he sat down beside her.

"They had to leave early. Jess's husband only let her come in the hope she'd win some money."

"Did she?"

"No, but Sally gave her ten pounds to keep him happy. I don't think he treats her very well."

Their conversation was cut short by a thunderous roar from the kitchen and the crackle and crash of breaking glass. They were silenced by the shock. What could be happening?

A second blast blew out the door behind the bar and a wall of heat rushed towards them. The kitchen seemed to be one enormous red furnace and black smoke began to fill the room.

The air was full of screams and the sound of people knocking over chairs and pushing madly at each other as they fought to get down the stairs. She knew she ought to move but she was mesmerised by the scene around her. Stiff with fright, she watched as if at a disaster movie.

"On the floor," shouted Al as he pulled Katie onto her knees, guiding her ahead of him as they crawled through the legs of the terrified customers. She could see Tania in front of her, also crouching low to avoid the smoke, and she began to cough as it reached her, stinging her eyes and making it hard to breathe.

Half falling, half stumbling, they reached the staircase. It was difficult staying upright on stairs that were only wide enough for two but where she was being squeezed by people trying to push past on either side. There were frantic cries coming from behind her and she had to put her hands out in front of her to stop herself being propelled forward. She could feel Al's hands on her shoulders as he protected her from the buffeting from above. Someone above her was shouting for help and she was sure she could hear another voice praying. It was all she could do to stay on her feet and she tumbled forward until her way was blocked by someone who had, indeed, fallen.

"Stop," she shouted but the force behind her was too great. She was flung across the body at her feet and a heavy boot crushed her arm.

She was crying now - not from fear of the fire – but because she knew she could be trampled to death. She thought of her mother, who had worked so hard to make up for her father's treatment of her. She thought of Heather – growing into a happy child who would make any parent proud – and she thought of Ned, who had drawn strength from her love and who still relied on her to interpret life for him. Would she ever see them again?

Strong arms lifted her clear and she could hear voices around her. Why couldn't she see? But she could breathe the cold night air. She was outside, with a painful arm but otherwise unhurt. Her eyes were streaming and she tried to blink away the tears. Gradually her vision returned. She took deep breaths and felt the people holding her release their grip.

"It's all right. The fire engine is here." It was Al's voice. She looked up and was vaguely aware of hoses turned on the blazing roof.

"Thank you, Al. You saved my life."

"It was Cameron really. He pulled us through the Bingo hall. We couldn't get out of the back door." Katie looked for Cameron but could not see him.

There was a thud from the first floor and sparks flew from the roof. "It's caving in!" someone shouted. Then there was a thunderous crash and sounds of splintering glass.

"We got out just in time," said a dishevelled Tania. "That must have been the big window."

Katie shuddered. She could still taste the smoke in her mouth and wondered about the person who had fallen in front of her. She was dimly aware of other choking victims being ushered towards a waiting ambulance.

Al put his arm round Katie's shoulders as they watched a fireman with breathing apparatus enter the building. Suddenly a dark bulk filled the doorway. It was Blogger – his bald head scarred and bleeding, his clothes ripped and scorched. In his arms he carried the limp body of Lee, the chef. Blogger staggered as the fresh air hit him and Katie could just see the streaks of tears on his blackened face before he tipped forward and was only saved by the swift action of two paramedics. Stretchers and blankets were produced and the two whisked away before anyone could go with them.

Police were taking names and addresses and Cameron was hovering in the background.

"They won't let us go to our cars. I think you'd all better come and spend the night at my place. It's not far."

"I must ring Lane's End," said Katie. "I daren't go home in this state."

"Do it when we get in the warm." Tania took hold of her arm. "It's all right – he's got plenty of room."

Katie looked for Al but he was talking on his mobile, to Blogger's relations, she supposed. She pulled her jacket round her – her confidence gone, suddenly she felt very small and vulnerable. Let someone else make the decisions, she thought. I just want to sleep.

"Are you all right with a lift?" asked Cameron when they reached the tall block of flats overlooking the sea front, "I'm on the top floor."

"Yes, thanks," replied Katie, "I'll lean on Al. All I need is a sit down." She watched as Cameron pushed a button labelled "P."

"It's the penthouse," whispered Tania. "You wait till you see it."

The lift doors opened onto a small lobby. Cameron slid a card through a box on the wall and the door next to it opened onto a vision of beige and white. Golden wall-lights seemed to come on automatically and delicate corn-coloured drapes slid together, obscuring the view of the sea.

"It's beautiful, Cam – like a show home," murmured Katie.

"That's what it was when I bought it."

"He's an estate agent," said Tania, proudly.

"How long have you lived here?" queried Katie, trying to think of anything rather than the ordeal they had just been through.

"About a year. Come and see the kitchen. Tania will make us all some tea. We've all had a bit of a shock."

Katie stroked the velvety furniture as she followed the rest of them into the kitchen. It was about as big as the whole ground floor at Lane's End and she sat down heavily on one of the chrome chairs surrounding the smoked glass table. The colour scheme was crimson and black and everything was spotlessly clean.

"Does anyone ever cook here?" asked Al.

"Yes. I do," said Cameron. "I'm afraid that isn't one of Tania's skills." He bent down and took a bottle from a cupboard just as Tania set a tray of mugs in front of them. "I'll get the milk," she said.

"And I've got the brandy. This will make us all feel better." He poured a generous measure into each mug of tea and handed Katie a bowl of sugar lumps.

"Go on," he urged, "It's what you need."

She drank it down, but it made her want to cry. "Where's the bathroom?" she asked.

"I'll show you," said Tania, "and your bedroom. Don't get upset, Katie."

"Will you ring Mum for me? I don't want her to hear me like this." Tears were streaming down her face and she could hardly speak for the choking feeling in her throat.

"Of course. Look, all the bedrooms have en-suite bathrooms. Would you like a bath? We need to look at that arm."

"I think it's just bruised. I'd like a bath. Will you stay with me, Tania?"

"If you want. Look, this is your room. What do you think?" She opened the door to a small lilac bedroom.

"It's beautiful" exclaimed Katie, "but I haven't got anything to wear in bed."

"I'll lend you a nightie. You run your bath and I'll go and fetch one. There's a towelling robe hanging up behind the door. By the way, it's a shared bathroom. I hope you don't mind."

"As long as no one else comes in while I'm in the bath."

"No. You are quite safe. Al will be in the next room but I'll keep him occupied until you're decent. That is what you want, isn't it?"

Katie nodded. At this precise moment she wanted nothing else but to be able to soak in a warm cloud of perfumed bubbles, forget all that had happened to them, climb into that enticing bed and relax into a dreamless sleep.

Instead of sending Katie to sleep the bath invigorated her and by the time Al knocked on her door, and entered with a tray, she had dried her hair with the hair drier Tania had brought with the nightdress, a silky coffee coloured full length slip, and felt ready for some supper.

"Honey sandwiches and hot chocolate with a twist," he grinned.

"Thanks Al, I'm starving."

"Do you mind me kipping next door?"

"Of course not. We're lucky Cam was so near. You look different. Have you had a bath, too?"

"Cam let me use his shower. I'll let you eat in peace and see you later. Good night."

Katie felt a pang of disappointment. So he'd rather be with Tania and Cameron than with her, would he? That told her. Still, it made it easier to stick to her resolution. She would finish her supper and be asleep by the time he'd finished talking to his friends.

She woke next morning luxuriating in the soft bed. She'd slept better than she had for weeks. Rubbing her eyes, she glanced round the little room. It seemed unused, like a hotel room, rather than a room in someone's home. The bathroom door was closed. Is that how she had left it?

She ran her hands through her hair and spread it out on the pillow. The sheets had a faint perfume – was it honeysuckle? Whatever it was she was reluctant to get up, especially if she had to dress in the clothes she had worn last night. Her hands slipped over the nightdress Tania had lent her – it was quite unlike the cotton T-shirts she usually wore. Her shoulders were bare and one strap had dropped down her arm – or had it been moved down?

Her mind was clawing at a memory – or a dream. She'd had fantasies about Al before – one she could still recall, when he pulled her back from the edge of a cliff and folded her in his arms. She had woken, still burning from the thrill of having his body next to hers to find that it was Ned she was cuddling and hated herself for the memory.

Had Al come to her bed in the night – or had she imagined him gently stroking her?

She shook her head. If she couldn't recapture the image, it hadn't really happened. Now she had to get up and get back home as soon as she could.

She had a swift wash and returned to see a tiny pair of flesh coloured lace pants and a matching bra draped over the back of a chair. Had they been there before? Delighted, she put them on – sorry that she had to cover them with her clothes from the previous day. The smell of smoke still lingered on her shirt and she hesitated before she opened the bedroom door and went along the corridor to the kitchen.

Tania was sitting at the table, a big mug of coffee in front of her and a big grin on her face. "Did they fit?"

"The undies? Yes – where did they come from?"

"I got them. I went out this morning and bought us each a set. Do you like them?"

"They're beautiful, Tania. How much do I owe you?"

"Nothing, you dope. Call it an early Christmas present. I've got a red set – but those ones looked more you. Do you want some coffee?"

"Yes, please. Where are the boys?"

"Cam's still in bed. Al went to see if he could get his taxi back."

"I'll have to find my car. What did my mother say?"

"Last night? She asked if we were all safe and sent

her love."

Katie was staring at the room as if she'd never seen it before. "Gosh, Tania, this is a fantastic flat. I don't know anyone else who lives like this."

Tania looked serious.

"I'm not the only one, you know."

"Girl friend?"

"Yes. He's got quite a stable. He calls me his favourite filly and makes me laugh with stories about the others. They don't last long. He gets bored easily."

"Don't you mind being compared to a horse?"

"It's not like that. He talks to me, Katie. He tells me things. Can you imagine - a man who treats you as if you were an important, valued, thinking being?"

"You'll be telling me next you discuss books."

"Not books – give me a break – but politics, what's happening in the world, fashion even."

"In bed, I suppose." Katie couldn't keep the sarcasm out of her voice.

"Sometimes. That's fine, I grant you – but that's not the only reason I see him. We just click, mentally. He's good for me, Katie."

Do we all need different things from different people the older we get? thought Katie. She hoped not. She missed Ned. Whatever his deficiencies she would love to feel his comforting presence now.

"What about Duane?" she asked.

"Duane's lovely – and he's perfect for Oliver, but he's not exactly romantic, and hardly a match for Cameron in the looks department."

"I suppose Cam is attractive – but he knows it. He's a bit too smooth for my liking, but very charming, I'll grant you."

It was just then that Prince Charming himself entered the room. Katie blushed. How much had he overheard?

"Hallo girls – what'll we have for breakfast – bacon and egg – toast and marmalade?"

"I'll just have one of those bananas please," said Katie. "Then I'll be off. Thank you very much for putting us up."

"I'll come with you," said Tania, "If you don't mind dropping me in the village. See you, love."

"Cheers, girls." He kissed Tania and patted Katie on the arm. She picked up her bag, now containing yesterday's underwear, and followed Tania to the lift.

5

It was wonderful to be enveloped in her husband's strong arms and feel the genuine emotion in his words.

"You're back, you're back," he mumbled, nearly crushing her as he lifted her off her feet to plant kisses on her face.

"Wait, Ned – let me down. I need to get changed. Hallo, Heather – Mummy's all right. There was no need to worry."

"We were fine once we knew you were safe," said Rose, taking her bag. "Come inside and tell us all about it."

"It was just a fire – in the kitchens. We got out down the stairs. There really wasn't any drama."

"Was anyone hurt?"

"Some. I'll tell you later." Her eyes flitted towards Heather. "A cup of tea would be nice."

Bernard had his arm round her shoulders and he steered her into the dining room. He didn't seem to want to lose contact with her and sat next to her, holding her hands.

"Daddy, come and watch my programme with me," called Heather.

Bernard looked sorrowfully at Katie.

"Go-on," she said, "We've got plenty of time to talk."

Hesitantly he let go of her and went into the lounge with his daughter.

As Rose stood in the doorway Katie tried to smile but instead she began to shake. She clasped her hands together to control them but her shoulders were shuddering and she suddenly felt unusually chilled.

"Oh, Mum," was all she could get out before Rose ran into the room and hugged her tightly.

"You go to bed, love. I'll bring you a hot drink."

"Wh-what's happening to me?"

"It's delayed shock. I'll help you upstairs. Come on, try to stand."

Katie obeyed, hanging on to her mother and watching each foot as she placed on the step. She felt peculiar – almost as if her body did not belong to her. Bed seemed like a haven. She undressed in a daze, shivered into her nightdress and crawled between the sheets.

For a while the bed shook as she fought her quivering body. Rose came to her as if in a dream and she cuddled the soft rubbery hot water bottle that she brought until she eventually fell asleep.

Sunday morning Katie felt weak and drained, but at least she was no longer shaking.

"I'm going to work tomorrow," she declared at breakfast. "I can't afford an extra week off."

There was no argument. Rose just said, "Well, let's enjoy today. I'm going to make the left-over green tomatoes into chutney. Do you want to help, Heather?"

The little girl seemed to ponder the question. "What you doing today, Daddy?"

"I've got more apples to pick and the toilet block to clean – but I'll be back for lunch."

Heather wrinkled her nose. "I'll stay with Nana," she said.

"Can I help you?" asked Katie, putting her hand on her husband's arm to get his attention.

Bernard beamed. "Sure, that would make it more fun."

Not exactly fun, thought Katie, but they would be together, doing something useful, sharing an experience. It wasn't much – but it was more than they had been doing for months.

She really needed the imminent holiday. She'd almost lost touch with her husband since they had moved to Lane's End. The thought that she might have been parted from him for ever made her grit her teeth and determine to appreciate all that she had to live for. Just to get away from Lane's End and have Ned and Heather to herself made her feel hopeful. At last she would feel like a wife and mother.

Bernard and Heather were almost uncontrollable with excitement. Bernard had been working hard collecting all the ripe apples. George had bought them an extra shed and set it up next to the garage. He had promised to take Pat away nearer Christmas and seemed happy to help out in the orchard for a week.

Although it was September the weather was mild and the little family took a taxi from the station to their flat.

"You come to see the lights?" asked the driver.

"I forgot they'd be up already," said Katie. "I'm sure we'll get out one evening. Isn't that great, Ned?"

"Are they special lights?"

"Oh, yes" answered the driver, "They don't have lights like ours anywhere else in the world. Your little one will love them – and you can have a ride on the tram."

"What's a tram?" asked Heather.

"It's like a bus – but it's on rails." Katie was staring out of the window. "Let's get ourselves settled first. Look – there's the sea."

The block of flats was on a corner, across the road from a narrow promenade and the beach. To one side was a row of shops and over the road from the other was a mobile home park.

"The key is with the lady in the newsagents," said Katie as the cases were lifted out of the boot. "You wait here and I'll fetch it."

Bernard paid the taxi driver and stood holding Heather's hand until Katie returned. She unlocked the front door and started up the stairs.

"We're on the first floor. Flat 3. Come on."

They opened another door and walked straight into a large sitting room. Two floor-length windows looked out over the beach. The room was painted white and the furniture looked soft and inviting.

Bernard hesitated, not knowing where to take the luggage.

"Put that down, love," Katie laughed. "Let's explore."

There were more surprises in the kitchen. A big box of groceries sat on the worktop and inside the fridge they found a litre of fresh milk.

"Look, Heather – Rice Crispies – we don't have to shop until tomorrow."

"Can I have some now?"

"I don't see why not. We'll have a cup of tea, unpack and then go and look at the sea. How's that for an idea?"

"I've found the bedrooms," called her husband. "This is really nice."

They followed the sound of his voice down the corridor and Katie smiled at the sight of her casually dressed husband in the Wedgwood blue bedroom with its King-sized bed and white voile curtains.

"This looks too elegant for us," said Katie. "Let's find your room, Heather."

The next door opened onto a room with pale tangerine walls and two single beds, each with an animal coverlet.

"I want to sleep on that one."

"That's a giraffe, don't you like the elephant?" Katie teased.

"Gee-raff," copied Heather.

"Right. Daddy will bring your case in. You come and wash your hands and get your cereal. I think the bathroom is across the corridor."

Later that evening, when Heather was in bed the two adults sat together on the sofa. Katie rested her head on Bernard's shoulder.

"I should do the washing up."

"Don't go, yet."

"I think this is going to be good, don't you, Ned?"

"Just being with you is always good."

Katie felt herself blush. She hadn't expected a remark like that from Ned. He usually found it so hard to say what he was thinking. She'd been such an idiot – taking him for granted. She would try to appreciate him more

– and show him that she still cared for him, because she
did, didn't she?

Next day it was Bernard who could hardly wait to get
down to the beach. He had his trunks on under his
joggers. They each had a big colourful beach towel and
Katie had made them a thermos of coffee.

"I hope the water's not too cold," she said as they went
down the stairs. "Heather, you are not to go in until I say
so."

The sun was shining and there were a few people
already setting up deckchairs and heading for the water.
They picked a spot and Katie stayed with Heather while
Bernard collected two deck chairs.

Once they were set up he stripped down to his trunks,
ran to the sea and plunged into the waves.

The cold water felt at first like ice on Bernard's skin
– but as he forged through the waves he seemed to melt
into them until he and the sea were one. He could feel the
tide pulling and stroking him and he dived to the sea bed,
glorying in the sense of harmony that swimming always
gave him. When he was in the water he was afraid of
nothing – life was manageable – he felt the power of the
sea and was part of it. Reluctantly he turned and struck
out for home.

"I want to go with Daddy," Heather was wailing.

Katie had taken her down to the water's edge to
paddle and they both started to splash him as he emerged.

"Was it cold?" asked Katie as they started up the
beach.

"Yes, at first."

"Daddy, my feet are all sandy!"

"Do you want to go back in the water?"

Heather looked at her mother, waiting for her permission.

"You take her," said Katie. "I'll watch."

"Come on then, little one." Bernard took his daughter's hand and walked, still dripping, back to the sea.

They weren't there long – Heather was too nervous to venture far out. Although Bernard was tempted to put her on his shoulders and wade out deeper he knew Katie would not approve.

A young boy was playing in a rock pool at the end of a groyne. He had a plastic boat and was pushing it across the pool, trying to make it sink. He was reaching for pebbles just as Heather walked by and his hand caused her to trip and almost fall.

"Sorry," he said, as Bernard caught her just in time.

"It's OK," responded Bernard, looking for Katie.

Another couple had set up their chairs near his family. The woman was short and slim with light brown hair and a bright yellow swimsuit. The man was tall and fair with spectacles that seemed to hide and distort his eyes so that Bernard could not tell where he was looking. His forehead was furrowed so that he seemed permanently puzzled.

"Ryan?" he called out as Heather and Bernard reached him.

"I'm here, Dad." The boy behind them shouted.

"Good. Don't go too far away."

As Bernard reached for a towel he realised Katie had moved her chair. She was now sitting next to the other woman and they seemed deep in conversation.

Heather ran up to them. "Is that your Ryan?" she interrupted.

"Yes," came the reply. "Did he upset you?"

"He's throwing stones."

"Oh – is he? Did he throw one at you?" The woman looked concerned.

"No. He's throwing them at a boat."

"That's just a game. Would you like to play?"

Heather looked taken aback. "I haven't got a boat."

"I'm sure John can find you one – but be careful. We don't want you getting sand in your eyes. Ryan – show the little girl how to play pirates."

John held out another toy boat and a bucket and spade. "You might encourage him to be a little more creative," he said gently.

Bernard watched as Heather sat down next to the boy. He was older that her, he guessed, but no taller. They began to dig a channel away from the pool towards the sea.

The two women were chatting again. He stretched out on the towel and looked at the sky, but the sun hurt his eyes. He needed some sun glasses, or a hat with a peak. Perhaps later on they could go shopping. He'd love to go back in the sea but he ought to watch the children. No-one else seemed to be taking an interest. Heather was giggling and Ryan was poking at something in the bucket.

He got up and walked down the beach towards them.

"Look," said Ryan, "We've got a crab."

The tiny crab was sharing the bucket with a strand of seaweed and an inch of water.

"What are you going to do with it?" asked Bernard.

"I'm going to show Mummy," said Ryan and the three of them started back up the beach.

It was natural, then, for the four adults to introduce themselves properly and form a group. John and Lisa Walsh were staying at the holiday park.

"We managed to get permission to take Ryan out of school as it was the only week the shop would let me go," Lisa explained. There was no mention of John's occupation. "Katie tells me you run a market garden."

"With Rose," said Bernard, "and we have a camp site."

"Can we go camping, Dad?" asked Ryan.

"Perhaps next year. Come and get dressed now, one holiday at a time."

"But I want to go in the sea."

John looked concerned. "You would say that now Mummy has got dry."

"I'll take him," said Bernard. "Do you want to come, Heather?"

"It's too cold."

"Fine. You stay with Mummy. Come on, Ryan."

"Is your real name Katherine?" asked Lisa.

"No, my parents christened me Katie, to go with Smith – but I'd rather be Kate. Katie sounds childish now. Were you always Lisa?"

"It's funny how people feel about their names, isn't it. I was named Elisabeth but I've always been called Lisa. Do you have a middle name?"

"Yes – but I don't like to tell anyone."

"Why?"

"It's Grace, and my father never stopped telling me it was a mistake."

"That's not fair. What you need is a confidence boost. How about leaving the men with the children this afternoon and booking a bit of pampering?"

"Like what?"

"Well, I promised myself a hair-do while I was here. I fancied going blonde. You could take auburn highlights. Come on, I dare you."

Katie laughed. She hadn't felt like this for years – as if she suddenly had permission to enjoy herself. It was wonderful to find someone who was so relaxed in her company and who wanted to share experiences with her. This holiday was going to be more fun than she'd expected. If only she could be fairer to Ned, it would be perfect.

Her thoughts were interrupted by the two swimmers. Ryan shook himself over his father – who jumped up and chased him across the beach.

"There they go again," sighed Lisa. "Why do boys always have to play fighting?"

Katie laughed. "That's one thing I don't have to put up with," but she recognised the feeling. There was a longing in Lisa's voice that echoed her own thoughts – not even a longing, more like envy. She looked over at where her husband was towelling himself down. Heather was sitting nearby, gossiping away, showing him some patterns she had made in the sand. They looked so self-contained – unaware of the world around them. She wanted to shout, "Hey, I'm here – I'm part of this family." Maybe Lisa was right – she should have a hair-do, smarten herself up a bit. She remembered guiltily how she had dressed her best for Al. She should do that for Ned. After all, she had packed the new underwear Tania had bought for her. All she had to be was a little bit braver.

"I'll do it," she said to her new friend. "Let's make it tomorrow."

Both families were on the beach next morning when the competition was announced. It was organised by the holiday camp as part of their entertainment programme but as it was sponsored by the local paper anyone was allowed to join in.

"The last grand sandcastle competition of the season," announced the celebrity from the local TV station. "Donate £1 to charity and get your application forms here. All entrants must be under 12 and there are prizes for first, second and third. Each castle can be built by up to six children. Judging will be at two o'clock. Watch out for the tide!"

"Can we build whatever we like?" asked Ryan, "or does it have to be a castle?"

"No – anything – a turtle, a spaceship, or even my lovely face," and he grimaced at the boy.

"I know, Dad, let's make a racing car – like the advert on TV where they make a car out of sweets."

"It would need to be big, so you and Heather could sit in it. We'll find a space. Bernard and I will make a pile for you and you can shape it."

"Is that allowed?" queried Katie.

"Sure. We're just consultants, aren't we, Bernard?"

Bernard was already digging a trench and smiled happily.

"Come on, Katie," said Lisa. "Let's leave the kids to it. We'll bring back some lunch – OK?"

"Fine. We've plenty to drink. You go and have fun."

"This is such a treat," said Katie as they wandered round a large store. "I never have time to browse in shops like this."

"Don't you ever go to London?"

"No. I don't seem to go anywhere except…" she paused. Dare she tell her new friend about Al?

"Go on," Lisa encouraged.

"You won't talk about me to John, will you?"

"Of course not. Anyway, he wouldn't be interested."

"Well, I did go to a show with someone I met at the Bingo."

"Bingo?"

"The bar above the Bingo actually. He was very charming and he did make a pass at me."

"What did you do?"

"Nothing. I told him to take me home."

"Is that all – what a let down. I thought it was going to be something really juicy."

"But I keep thinking of him. I feel so disloyal. How can I make it up to Ned?"

"Do you still – you know?"

"Not very often. The novelty has worn off."

"Have you tried varying it – taking the lead?"

"You mean - " Katie blushed. She couldn't bring herself to put in to words what she was imagining.

Lisa was smiling. "We take turns, and we're about the same weight. I should think you'd appreciate a change as Ned's so much heavier than you."

Kate giggled. "I'll let you into a secret. A girl friend bought me some new underwear and I brought it with me. I was hoping it would help me feel more attractive."

"What a terrific idea. Now we'd better get our hair done and give the lads a real surprise."

It was gone one when the two women, loaded with crisps, sausage rolls and a pot of salad arrived back at the beach.

At first all they could see was John, sitting in a deck chair, guarding the sand car. Then they spotted Bernard and the two children down by the water's edge.

"Hi, John. What are they doing?"

"Getting pebbles for the headlights. What do you think?" He gestured towards the sandcastle.

"It looks very realistic. Are you sure you didn't help?"

"No. The judges came round while we were supervising. It's all above board. He leaned forward, staring at his wife. "You look different."

"It's platinum blonde. Do you like it?"

"Well, I'd soon find you on a dark night. It's a bit Marilyn Monroe isn't it?"

Lisa giggled.

"Mummy, see me sit in the car," shouted Heather as the others came running back.

"Careful," said John. "Don't jump in. It might collapse."

"Aw, Dad, it's too well made for that" Ryan quickly got into the driver's side. "Look at all the instruments. We made them with shells."

"Come and wipe your hands and have something to eat before they declare the results."

Ryan placed the pebbles Bernard handed him over the shapes for the lights. It really was quite impressive, thought Katie as they sat and munched the food she had bought.

"Tomorrow I'll make a proper picnic," she said. "Now I've found the supermarket."

"Shh, the judges are back. Get in the car, kids."

The two children sat proudly in the sand car as the judges approached with a photographer.

"And what kind of car is this, young man?" asked one.

"A Ferrari," declared Ryan.

"Very good – and how old are you?"

"I'm six and Heather is nearly four."

"Excellent. You make a very pretty picture."

As they moved away Ryan asked, "Will our photos be in the paper, Dad?"

"Perhaps. If you win a prize."

A crowd gathered to hear the results. Third place went to a mermaid, second was the Ferrari and as they collected their bags of goodies, balls, books, toys and sweets the delighted children were almost too absorbed to hear the announcement of the winner – a giant octopus.

They were packing away their belongings when a breathless young man came up to them. "Can you give us your full names, please, for the paper?"

"Heather Longman and Ryan Walsh," said Katie.

"Good. You should be in Thursday's edition. All the winners will be featured, although the octopus has just drowned," and he waved towards the sea. Sure enough, a few of the entries were now being swallowed up by the incoming tide.

"Ours won't be here in the morning," said John. "But you did well, troops. Come on, time we made tracks."

That night Katie changed into her new bra and pants and then covered them with her nightie. Her heart was thumping and she felt a mixture of excitement and trepidation. Was this really a stupid idea or would it bring back a little of the romance in their lives?

Bernard returned from checking on Heather.

"She's fast asleep," he said, his voice full of affection. "This is going to be a good holiday." He paused, focussing at last on her hair. "You've had a haircut!"

"And you've only just noticed."

"It's shining under the light. It's very pretty."

"Thanks, darling. I'm just going to clean my teeth." She scuttled past him to the bathroom.

I can't do it, she thought. I can't act like someone else. He'd think I was ridiculous – going to bed in underwear. She undressed, rolled the precious garments into a ball and replaced her nightdress. There was still one experiment she was determined to try and she could do that in the dark.

Bernard was lying on his back – his head propped up by his arms. Katie turned the light off and crawled in beside him. Then she turned and unbuttoned his pyjama jacket.

Resting her head on his chest she wrapped her arms around him. The silence halted her. She waited for a response.

Bernard bent forward and kissed the top of her head, his hands feeling for her, stroking her back through the nightdress. She reached up and pulled it over her head and then moved his hands down, indicating that he, too, should be naked.

Still he said nothing but looking into his eyes she thought she could see surprise and delight.

She bent down to kiss him and he held her tightly. Now she could, at last, show him how much he meant to her.

Afterwards they lay together – she with one leg across him and he panting and looking triumphant.

Katie felt the impulse to giggle. She could sense the smile on his face.

"I love you," he said, simply.

"That worked, didn't it?" She didn't really need reassurance but she felt so happy she had to say something.

"Katie, my Katie." He turned and cuddled her.

She shivered. "We'd better get covered up." Thank you, Lisa, she thought – thank you for making me brave enough to try something new.

All the tension in her body seemed to have drained away. She felt ready to enjoy herself again. There was no more guilt, no more secrets, just the feeling of gratitude that she was part of such a loving family.

The rest of the week flashed by in a whirl of enjoyment. They rode the trams, marvelled at the lights, climbed the tower and spent hours on the beach.

One day the Walsh's invited them into the camp and they used the pool, had a meal in the restaurant and watched a show. Heather tried hard to keep up with Ryan but she fell asleep while the music was playing for dancing and Bernard took her back to the flat. To his surprise John came too, his only explanation, "I'm not much of a dancer."

Once Heather had been settled the two men sat down together.

"I want to thank you, Bernard," John began. "You and Katie have made our holiday such fun."

Bernard was puzzled. He didn't feel he'd done anything unusual. He'd played with the children and Katie had talked to Lisa. They'd shared sandwiches and drinks. What could his friend mean?

"Katie has been like a breath of fresh air to Lisa. She was so tired and irritable before we came away. It's such a strain when I can't work."

"You haven't a job?"

"No, I've tried – but my eyesight is now so poor there is little I can do. I can't even do voluntary work in case I make a mistake. I can't see a computer screen, I can't drive a car, I find reading difficult. I'm not blind and yet my vision is so restricted. Ryan is growing up and I can't even play football or cricket with him, or even watch a match properly."

"But you can see him?" Bernard found it difficult to imagine such a condition.

"Yes – when he's at the right distance. It's like looking through a tunnel. It makes a lot of extra work for Lisa."

Bernard didn't know how to respond. Only one person had ever spoken to him in this manner, his friend Zak. Thinking of Zak gave him an idea.

"I know somewhere that might help you," he said, delightedly. "I learnt to be a gardener at a college. I stayed in the week and went home weekends."

"I couldn't do that."

"No – that's not what I mean. They asked me to go back at weekends when they opened for other people – people in wheelchairs, blind people- people with different problems."

"What did they do?"

"Everything, painting, writing, woodwork, they're the ones I helped, sewing, computing, acting, making music – I'm sure there would be something you'd like."

John was smiling at his enthusiasm. "How do I find this paradise?" he joked.

Bernard frowned. "You mean the college?"

"Yes. Is it near you?"

"I had to go on a train – but not many hours. I'm sorry;

85

you'll have to ask Katie."

He was serious now, but pleased that he could be useful to someone without the help of his wife or his mother-in-law.

"I will. If there's something I could learn that would help me find employment I'd be willing to give up my weekends. I must go now – the dancing will be over. I'll bring Katie back. Thanks, Bernard."

They shook hands and John left Bernard to puzzle over the happenings of the week. He felt, somehow as if there had been another change in his life – a step forward – but a step into the unknown.

He and Katie had become a team again. If only this would last when they got back to Lane's End.

6

Rose hadn't expected to feel so at peace when her family went on holiday. She missed them, of course, but having the house to herself – rather than making her feel lonely – gave her an unaccustomed feeling of freedom. In fact she felt younger, almost mischievous.

She tried to tell Pat how she felt. "It's such a change, not having anyone to cook for – not having to watch out for Heather all the time. I was feeling old, Pat – but today I feel full of energy. Do you know what I would really like to do?"

"Go shopping?"

"Yes – in a way. I want to choose another dog."

"Oh, Rose. You know Katie wasn't keen on Heather having a pet until she was old enough to take care of it."

"This isn't for Heather. It's for me. I want a dog. I won't decide without the rest of the family but I'm going to put my name down at the rescue centre. I want to see what they have. It doesn't have to be a pedigree."

"So that's why you agreed to the wall. You'd better get

something that can't jump too high."

"I intend to train it – but it will live indoors. I never really liked Jenny being outside in a kennel."

"She was a working dog. You're softer than you look, Rose Smith."

"There's something else I've done. I've turned Tim's office into a study. If Bernard gets a computer I can use it for the accounts and he can do his writing in peace."

"My – you have come alive this week, haven't you?"

"Yes. I'm going to the animal shelter this afternoon. Would you like to come with me?"

"Just to stop you falling in love. I'd be glad to."

"Right. I'll pick you up when you close. I can't see that they'd turn me down. We've always had dogs."

"Can I help you, ladies?" smiled a young woman as they entered the foyer.

"We've just come for a look round," said Rose, "But we'd also like information on how to adopt."

"You know we have to inspect the proposed home?"

"Yes."

"Well, do look round and we'll have the forms ready for you when you come out."

Rose led Pat through the double doors and into a corridor. On each side were cubicles with glass fronts and by each window a label giving the age and character of the dog inside.

Some of the dogs were barking and Rose's eye was taken by a small black terrier that was leaping at the glass.

"That dog would suit us," she said, "and it might scare off unwanted visitors."

"Oh, look," said Pat, pointing to a bedraggled lurcher.

"Doesn't he look in need of a good home?"

"I've got to find something that won't frighten Heather," said Rose. She paused to read the details of a rusty brown dog curled up at the back of the cubicle.

Sandy. A three year old collie/spaniel bitch. She has suffered violence in the past but has a gentle nature.

The dog was looking at her and she called out to it.

"Sandy, how are you Sandy?"

It gave a single thump of its feathery tail and Rose succumbed.

"If that is still here when I come back – I'm taking it," she declared.

"Don't you want to see the rest?"

"No. Let's go and arrange the inspection. If they can come this week I can have her home before Katie gets back."

"You weren't going to get one until they'd seen it."

"It will be my dog. I'm sure they'll love it. I've missed having a dog. It really is the perfect place for one."

Lane's End passed with flying colours and Friday morning Rose was back, eager to take charge of her new dog.

"We need to see you together," said the assistant. "We'll bring her on the lead and you can take her for a walk."

Rose hadn't felt so excited and apprehensive for years but instinct told her that Sandy was destined to come to her.

The dog didn't pull on the lead. It looked nervously at the young girl as she handed her over. Immediately Rose started to talk to her. Soothingly she repeated her name.

"Good dog, Sandy. You're going to like coming home

with me," she murmured. The dog's eyes were fixed on her face – her tail slowly beginning to swish from side to side. Her gingery ears were feathered like her tail and her back was streaked with black. She was the most beautiful dog Rose had ever seen. She squatted down, let the dog sniff her hand and then ran it over her back. The dog shivered but stood still and then reached up to lick Rose's face.

"What does she have to eat?" asked Rose as she wrote the cheque.

"Everything is in the folder," replied the girl. "She's had all her injections. She's not able to have puppies. I would suggest dry meal to start with."

"Does she like toys?"

"She may well do – once she's begun to relax. Keep her on the lead near sheep until you know how she reacts."

The dog whined softly when the van started up but Rose talked to her all the way back and she seemed to calm down. When they reached Lane's End she kept her on the lead until they had got through the new gate into the private area. The dog seemed reluctant to leave her side and sniffed at the hedge before watering the grass and following Rose through the front door. Once inside she ran from room to room as if she was searching for something, or someone.

Rose patted the dog bed she had placed at the end of the kitchen – but the dog hid under the table and she had to coax her out with some treats.

"I do hope you aren't going to be too timid," she told her. "One of the reasons I wanted a dog was to guard the house."

She made a sandwich and tea and moved into the lounge. The dog followed and curled up at her feet.

"That's better. After lunch I'll take you to see Pat. I'm going to need some support when the others get back."

Saturday afternoon Rose, uncertain about leaving the dog in the house on her own, left Sandy with Pat and went to the station to collect the family.

As they were piling the cases into the boot Katie said,

"Where's the old travel rug, mum?"

"I've got another use for it. We can get a new one."

"What use?"

"We've got a dog. I left the blanket with Pat so that it had something soft to sit on."

"The dog's with Pat?"

"Yes, but she's ours."

"What do you mean – OURS! You promised not to get a dog until Heather was older."

A flash of guilt made Rose's face redden.

"I didn't want anyone else to have her. She's called Sandy."

"Is it a poodle-dog?" asked Heather.

"No, she's not. She's a brown collie, with spanielly ears – you'll love her."

Katie was silent.

"Is she like Jenny?" asked Bernard.

"Not really. She's a bit shy."

"Oh, that's all we need," snarled Katie. "A wimp of a dog that we have to mollycoddle."

"Wait till you meet her," said Rose grimly. "Did you have a nice holiday?"

"It was lovely." Katie's voice softened. "And we met a

really great family. We promised to keep in touch."

"Did you like it, Heather?"

"Yes – and we won a prize!"

"They made a sandcastle," explained Bernard. "Then Heather and Ryan had their photographs taken for the paper."

"Right. We'll get inside and get sorted and then I'll take you down to Pat's."

"I'll stay and unpack," said Bernard. "You all go."

Pat was beaming when they arrived at the shop. "She's been very good," she said, "and look, she sits on command." But Sandy was weaving round Rose's legs.

"Can I stroke her?" asked Heather.

"Yes, if I can keep her still."

The dog allowed herself to be stroked and then jumped up at Rose.

"You'll have to train her not to do that, Mum," said Katie.

"I will – but isn't she lovely?"

"She's a nice looking dog. Well. You've done it now. Let's go home. I'm really tired."

"Can I hold her lead?" asked Heather.

"Not yet, darling. When we know her better. She might get frightened by something and pull you over."

They were all sitting round the dining table when Bernard came downstairs. As soon as he entered the room there was a low growl from under the table.

"Is that the dog?" asked Bernard and bent to look between the chairs.

Immediately Sandy began a paroxysm of barking. She stood up and backed away, barking furiously.

"Oh dear," said Rose. "She seems afraid of you, Bernard."

Bernard backed away, looking concerned. "What can I do?" he said.

"Ignore it," suggested Katie. "Pretend it isn't here. It will settle."

He gingerly pulled out a chair and sat down. The dog continued barking but did not approach him.

"Quiet, Sandy," ordered Rose and the barking turned to a throaty growl.

"I think you are right, Katie. They did say she had been mistreated. I expect she's scared of men."

"Well, that will have to change. Don't worry, Heather."

The little girl was standing, white faced, in the doorway. She looked poised to run out of the room.

"It's all right, Heather. She likes you. She'll get used to Daddy if he doesn't hurt her."

"I wouldn't," said Bernard. "I'm sorry, Rose. Shall I eat in the lounge?"

"Certainly not. If I could shut the dog in the kitchen I would, but with no door she'll just have to get used to you. If she's too much of a nuisance I'll put her in the porch."

"No, don't do that, Mum," said Katie. "Give it time." Turning to Bernard she continued, "Ned, if we want to go to the children's playground before it closes for the winter we ought to go tomorrow. Once I get back to work it won't feel like a holiday anymore."

The change of subject seemed to satisfy her husband. He got up carefully and went towards the back door. "I'll just have a look round," he said as he put on his Wellingtons and went out.

The dog, silent now, followed Rose into the kitchen looking hopeful.

"You don't get any treats until you learn to be good with Bernard," scolded Rose.

Sandy wagged her tail.

"Katie, let this dog out into the front, will you? She might as well get used to the place."

Katie did as suggested and her daughter ran ahead of her into the garden.

Heather found a ball and threw it for the dog. At first she chased after it but seemed to lose interest when she reached it. Instead her attention was caught by something in the corner of the garden.

Through the wire mesh of the run she could see the chickens. One flew up to its little wooden hut. Sandy leapt forwards and ran round the coop looking for a way in.

The chickens went wild with fright. They clucked and flapped, pecking at each other in an effort to get inside, away from the dog. Sandy let out a sharp bark and seemed to watch for a reaction from the chickens. There was frantic activity in the coop and Sandy ran at the netting, yapping delightedly.

Katie and Rose came running out of the house.

"No, Sandy, no," shouted Rose as Katie managed to grab her collar and pull her away.

Heather was standing, horrified, and near to tears.

"That's another problem," said Katie, dragging the dog indoors. "Now we'll have to move the chickens."

"It never occurred to me. They must think she's a fox," said Rose.

"It isn't what they think – it's what the dog might do. I expect she just wanted to play, but we can't risk it. That's enough excitement for one day. Come on, precious – time for bed."

The next morning Bernard cleared a space in the orchard and transferred the chickens to their new home. It left an untidy patch on the lawn but Rose had the answer. "We'll fence off a corner of the garden for Sandy, so she doesn't do her business everywhere. It will feel like the kennels to her, her own patch. I'm going to get one of those extending leads and a squeaky toy. She needs lots to do."

"And lots of attention," grumbled Katie. "Right, everyone, are we ready for our trip?"

The children's playground had only a few families inside. Most of the parents were in the little café watching while their children ran from the helter-skelter to the cage of balls and then on to the miniature train.

"Can I go on the train, Mummy?" asked Heather.

"Of course. Daddy and I will sit here and watch you."

There were only two other children on the train which went round in a circle with bells clanging and whistle blowing. It wasn't as sophisticated as the fair they had been to on holiday but Heather looked just as happy.

When the train stopped, two adults came out of the café towards the boy and girl who clambered down behind Heather. The man who picked up the young boy and swung him onto his shoulder looked familiar to Katie.

"How was that, Harry?" he asked.

Katie froze. Her fists clenched and her heart hammered. The man was Al.

She watched the woman put her arm through his and then bend to say something to the girl. The two of them moved off towards the toilets. Al hadn't seen her and she felt like hiding. Where could she go?

Bernard hadn't noticed anything was wrong. He was helping Heather off with her shoes so that she could go on the big slide.

Katie moved towards the café, but as she did so Al turned and spotted her. The boy wriggled and he put him down on the ground. Giving her a sheepish grin Al let himself be dragged towards the bouncy castle. The boy flung off his trainers and leapt on. Once alone Al walked back towards her.

"So you've found me out?" he said breezily.

"They're your children?" Any fragment of hope that he might just be with a friend vanished with the reply.

"Yes, Harry and Deborah. Carol is with Debs."

"You didn't tell me."

"You didn't ask."

"I'm glad I know now," and as she said it, she realised the truth. However attractive Al had seemed to her it was only superficial attraction – she hadn't really known anything about him.

"Can we still be friends?"

She smiled. "I don't see why not. I'll see you around," and she walked swiftly away. Her jaw felt tight and she was gritting her teeth but her shoulders were straight and she was determined not to look back. She needed to breathe the sea air, get this choking feeling out of her throat and the rising anger that she had been duped. She'd been so easy to deceive – so ready to be charmed – thank goodness she'd found out about him in time, before she'd done anything really stupid. She stood on the pebbles and took great gulps of sea air. The holiday had shown her what was important to her. Now she had to focus on getting back to work.

She couldn't wait to get away from the playground

and back to Lane's End.

"Where were you?" asked Bernard when she returned.

"I went to look at the café."

"Do you want a drink?"

"No, thank you. I'm sorry, Ned. I don't feel too well. Can we go home?"

"Of course. I'll get Heather."

Heather's disappointment was alleviated when Bernard promised they would take Sandy for a walk when they got back.

Katie was glad not to have to offer an explanation. How could she feel anger and relief at the same time? She wanted to be sick and had the strangest sense that once she had done so she would be rid of the feelings she had for Al for ever. She had come back from the holiday cheerful and optimistic and now he had shaken her judgement. How could she have been such a fool? Why hadn't she guessed Al was married? He'd looked happy with his family, but it seemed one woman was not enough for men like him and Cameron.

She made a new resolution – to make the best of the life she had. After all, she had so much to be thankful for.

7

James Longman took one last look round the shop before he switched off the lights and locked the door. Victor could manage without him now the summer season was over.

He always enjoyed his three months helping to sell the outdoor clothing and camping equipment. The Lake District was his favourite part of the country – but now he had to get back to his real job. The guest houses and hotels along the west coast liked him to do their decorating in the winter months, although he had to leave Blackpool itself until the early spring.

He was lucky that Victor had bought him the campervan so that he didn't have to stay in one place. He could travel to wherever the work was.

He dropped the keys through Victor's letterbox and strolled round to his home on wheels. The arrangement he had with Victor suited them both. It allowed James to feel free and untraceable. He let himself into the campervan and went through to the bathroom. His grey hair was still in a ponytail and he shook it out and combed it through. He'd have a shower and then get something to eat. Tomorrow he'd motor down the coast.

His usual parking space was still available when he reached the town and he wandered round to the supermarket and bought some milk and a local paper. He'd probably have to put in a new advertisement – just to show he was around – but he did have two regular customers who liked him to spruce up their guest rooms for the Christmas trade.

Back home, lounging with a cup of coffee he scanned the headlines until he noticed the wording under a set of photographs.

There had been a local sandcastle competition and the winning entries were pictured with the children who built them. Under the picture of a boy and girl sat in a sand car were the words, *Ryan Walsh and Heather Longman in their Ferrari.*

The name Longman jumped out at him. He was a Longman. Could this little girl be related to him?

He was surprised at the feeling of hope it gave him – until he remembered his son. There was no way Bernard could have fathered such a beautiful, intelligent looking child – or was there? If he'd lived this long he'd be the right age.

James tried to pull himself together. After all – he'd been quite content on his own for 25 years. What was the point in wondering about his wife and child now?

He spent the next morning discussing colour schemes

with a customer. Normally this would have given him a sense of satisfaction but when he arrived home the paper was still open at the page with the sandcastle competition.

It wouldn't hurt him to look in the local phone book, would it? He'd drop into the library and check it out – just to satisfy himself.

There were no Longmans in the local phone directory and he knew he'd feel too much of a fool phoning anyone in the rest of the country. He needed to find out where the girl came from. She must have been a visitor. Perhaps she gave her address to the local paper? Now he'd started searching he didn't want to give up. There was something about her face. The least he could do was ask the paper for a copy of the photo.

Once he had made the decision he felt energised. The young woman assistant in the newspaper office was more helpful than he'd expected and, once he'd ordered the photograph, called the features team to find out if they had any more information.

"One of the kids came from Durham and the other from Sussex. That's all I know," was the reply.

Which was which? James's heart beat faster. There was a chance, just a slim chance, that the girl could be his granddaughter. He couldn't believe how much it was beginning to matter to him. His emotions had been closed down for so long. He'd told himself that he was happier alone. He'd made friends and enjoyed the company of a few women, but he'd not loved anyone since he'd left Anne in their home by the Downs.

He could visualise it now – part of a modern terrace outside – but with his personal signature inside. The kitchen had been blue and white, with a cornflower pattern on the tiles. The big room had been coffee coloured with a rich rust carpet and their bedroom had been dove grey and burgundy. He'd so enjoyed decorating their home, and the lemon yellow bedroom with the animal frieze that he'd designed for their first child, James Bernard Longman. His mood changed as he remembered their son and the hopes and dreams that had been shattered when the boy started school.

At first he had just seemed a quiet lad. He was tall, like his father, but big boned and clumsy. Anne adored him and James was glad that he'd made her so happy. Then it became apparent that school bewildered the child. He did not want to attend. He did not seem able to remember his lessons and had difficulty holding a pencil.

James became more and more irritated by his son's lack of progress and enraged by his wife's attitude. "It doesn't matter," she would say. "He's ours and we love him."

But James did not love him – in fact he was beginning to hate him. Why did he have to have a son like that? Was it something in his genes – or something he had done? He'd spent years on the sheep farm. Could that have affected him? And why on earth had they called him James? The child seemed to sense his father drawing away from him and when the rows started would run to his mother and hide behind her.

"Don't shout at me in front of Bernie," she would say, as if the words he spoke were nothing. He couldn't argue with her. He didn't know how to resolve the situation – so he left.

They'd been on a caravan holiday in the West Country – the kind of place where boys climb trees and go fishing. By then they were both calling young James, "Bernard" and James had made one last effort to make friends with his son.

"I'll draw something in the sand," he said, "and you can tell me what it is."

"Plane," said Bernard.

"Good. Now I'll write its proper name underneath and you can read it."

He wrote aeroplane carefully under the drawing. Even if the child hadn't seen the word before he thought he'd have a guess. At the very least he was certain he'd repeat plane.

"I want to go in the water," responded Bernard.

"When you've told me what that says."

Bernard's face wrinkled and tears came into his eyes. "I don't know," he whimpered.

"You DO know," shouted James. "You've just told me!"

"Mummy," called Bernard and ran back to his mother.

That night James left a note and went home. He packed a few things, took one last look round the house he had loved and took a train to London. He'd wanted to make sure he could not be found – and he'd done it.

He trusted that Anne would manage. She had friends in the library and the church. The rent on the house was fixed. If he was right and the boy was brain-damaged he probably wouldn't live past his early teens. They would both be better off without him.

That's how he'd thought for all these years – and now what was it that was driving him to find them? What would Anne look like now? he wondered. Would she have found someone else? Had she forgiven him? Did she still live in their old home?

He'd never wanted to admit to himself that he'd been a coward. He had found it impossible to go through

102

every day with a child who seemed to find the simplest things in life difficult. Was it because he suspected his own mother may have been a non-reader? She'd never shown any interest in books or learning. He felt, as the much younger son, he had been a mistake – but he hadn't wanted his own child to feel like that.

Did anyone get all they wanted out of life? he thought. Had Anne found happiness without him and had Bernard really fathered a child – a beautiful, bright child that made James want to see her for himself?

He couldn't afford to leave the west until Christmas. Perhaps if he took a week off then and drove to the coast some of those questions could be answered. He wouldn't have to declare himself, just watch and see if the little girl really was his granddaughter.

He walked slowly home – looking in shop windows. It was time to buy some more jewellery. He didn't have a bank account – just a private locker – and his savings were all in gold and diamonds. It was something he and Anne had had in common – a love of jewellery. He remembered choosing their wedding rings, engraved golden bands which promised togetherness, a promise he had broken.

He'd concentrate on the wallpaper design for "Belle View." The landlady said she wanted regency stripes – not his favourite – but perhaps he could find a modern take on it. The carpet was patterned. Didn't she realise that would have to change?

His fingers began to ache – please, not arthritis, not yet – he still had many years of working life ahead of him, didn't he?

By December Katie had made two important discoveries.

One – Heather's hearing, although not perfect – was at an acceptable level.

Two – Katie was pregnant.

She tried to work out when the baby had been conceived. It would have been after she had recovered from her illness but before they returned from holiday. Could the anti-biotics have upset her rhythm – or had she been so intent on mending her marriage that she had missed taking precautions for a few days?

She could not admit to herself that she had done it deliberately but now it had happened she was bursting with happiness.

It would be good for Heather to have a sibling and this time they should be able to bring up their child without interference. Losing her daughter for a year of her life had been devastating, and rebuilding trust had drained her of energy. She'd managed it, thanks to toddler club, but she was sure she would be more relaxed with a second child.

She'd like another girl to be a playmate for Heather but if it was a boy she would be just as content. Only one tiny doubt remained. What if he looked like Al?

She'd successfully subdued all memory of the night at Cameron's flat – but now there could be a possibility, however remote – that something did happen – she needed to find out – or did she? Had she the nerve to question him now she knew he had a wife and children – and would he tell her the truth?

She realised with sudden certainty that he would not. He would deny that he had come to her bed, and she would look a complete idiot for suggesting it. There was no way she could tell him. She would just have to wait, and pray. It must be Ned's baby. It was a holiday baby. I'm sure of it, she told herself.

The question of Heather's hearing test seemed unimportant in comparison but she had been asked a question that felt significant.

"How is your hearing?" said the nurse, "And your husband's?"

Katie was about to reply, "Fine," when she hesitated. Ned didn't always hear what was said to him. She'd got so used to standing in front of him to talk to him that she'd not registered it as unusual. He could never hear what she said in a crowd and often did not reply when she was driving him somewhere.

"I don't think my husband's hearing is 100%," she said.

"Well, perhaps he'd better get it tested. I'll make an appointment."

Katie put the card in her bag. "Thanks, nurse. Come on, Heather. We'll go in the park before we go home."

James drove past the King's Head and into the town. It looked about the same. There were a few new houses just back from the main road and a new mini roundabout. Every now and then a house was decorated with coloured lights, snowmen and Santas. He remembered the Christmas he'd been the happiest, when his son was about three and they'd had a big tree with coloured baubles that Bernard kept trying to pull off.

James had bought him a train that went round in a circle and at first Bernard enjoyed watching it but his eyes lit up at the sight of patterned wrapping paper and they ended up folding it into shapes. He'd seemed to have everything a man could want, then, but it didn't last.

He pulled up by the churchyard and walked back to his old home. It had blue lights like rain dripping from the roof, and a different front door.

He swallowed hard. His collar felt strangely tight.

The curtains were closed but there was music coming from inside. How could he find out if his family were still there? He'd come all this way. There was nothing for it but to knock and ask. He could feel his palms sweating as he reached for the bell. It rang once, twice, three times before a man's voice called out, "All right, I'm coming."

The door opened and a bearded face greeted him.

"Oh, it's not carol singers. Can I help you?"

"I was looking for Mrs Longman," blurted James, feeling his face redden. "She used to live here."

The man turned away from him. "Dora – what happened to Mrs Longman?"

A slim, mousy haired woman came to the doorway. "I'm sorry. Are you a relative?"

"Yes. I take it they moved?"

"Not exactly. I'm afraid she died in an accident – some years ago. She was knocked down in the street. I'm awfully sorry."

James suddenly felt cold. His legs felt weak under him and he held onto the door frame to stop himself falling. "She died?" he heard himself repeat. "She's really dead?"

"Yes. I think she was cremated. She had a son, didn't she?"

"Yes. Was he with her?"

"No – but I couldn't tell you what happened to him. They might know up at the vicarage. Would you like to sit down, or have a drink of water?"

James realised he must have gone pale but he couldn't stay at the house any longer. He could see the colour scheme in the hall had changed, a visible symbol of the way time had moved on and left him behind.

"I'm OK. I'll go and see the vicar," he mumbled and hurried down the path. He needed to get back in his van and away from this place as fast as he could. He should never have come. Once inside he opened a bottle of whisky and drank two glasses to steady himself.

He needed time to assimilate all he had learned. He hoped Anne hadn't suffered – but in a sense she had been dead to him for years. There was no point in mourning now. Of course it had been a shock. He'd been prepared to find her older, perhaps with white hair – but he hadn't expected to find she had passed away.

It seemed possible that the boy was still alive, perhaps in some institution. Should he at long last accept his responsibilities and help towards his care? He couldn't go back just yet. He'd stay a few days and see how he felt. He might even go to church at Christmas.

James needed a distraction. He'd not let his emotions surface for years and now he could hardly control the turmoil in his head.

He usually found refuge in music, especially folk music, and everywhere he travelled he tried to find the local folk club and relax in the welcoming atmosphere that always prevailed. Among such company he belted out sea shanties in a rich baritone that belied his slim frame with its light blue eyes and long hair. Sheep farming had never been his thing and he liked to believe he was descended from sailors or fishermen from the North East.

But he didn't feel like company tonight. He didn't want to perform, just listen, and get lost in the music.

He switched on a familiar CD. The music soothed him and he began to relax. Nothing had changed. His life could still go on as before. There was nothing to worry about – yet.

8

"Would you be pleased if Heather was to have a little brother or sister?" asked Katie.

Bernard looked as if he was struggling to understand her meaning.

"I think we are having another baby," she explained. "I'm pregnant, Ned."

Bernard's face broke into a wide smile. "Another baby?" he echoed. "Have we really made another baby?"

"Yes,darling. It's due in the summer. Won't that be great?"

Bernard grabbed her and swung her round and then stopped, suddenly concerned.

"Should I have done that?" he asked.

"I'm not bone china," she laughed and then continued giggling as she saw the puzzled look on his face.

"I mean, I won't break easily," she said. "I'm not fragile."

"Does Rose know?"

"Yes. She guessed – but I wanted to tell you when Heather wasn't around. It's too soon to tell her, Ned.

Little children expect everything to happen so quickly. She wouldn't understand waiting months."

"I mustn't tell her?"

"No – not until I get really fat. Then we'll tell her."

"That will be hard."

"I know. You can tell Chantelle, but make sure she knows it's a secret, and you can write to Zak."

"I will. Oh, Katie – it might be a little boy this time."

"Let's wait and see. Gosh, I forgot how excited you were when this happened last time." But she was excited, too. She'd have to telephone Lisa and give her the good news.

James came out of church uplifted by the carols. A lady vicar? That was a turn up for the books. He didn't really feel comfortable with it – but she had been very authoritative and talked a load of sense. He'd asked her after the service if she knew what had happened to Bernard and she'd promised to enquire.

He wouldn't go back now, not until she gave him some sort of answer. When the library opened after the holiday he'd pop in there. It was all such a long time ago.

Once James was in the library he realised he might be able to find out what happened to Anne in the reference section. He felt he owed it to her to learn as much as he could about the circumstances of her death. Eventually he found the article in a back copy of the local paper and saw the appeal for Bernard.

"I can look on the computer and find more references for you, if you like?" suggested the librarian.

"Thanks – I'm not really into computers," muttered James.

"There – two references – but they are for Ned Longman – one about a mosaic and another about a sensory garden. Could he be a relative?"

James was puzzled. Who was Ned Longman? It couldn't be Bernard, could it?

Apparently this person had helped an old lady design something for the harbour museum and built a pantomime wall for a school garden. This he would have to see. He raced back to the van. If it was his son - could he be artistic even if he couldn't read or write? He'd never seemed to listen to what he was told, at least, not when James had spoken to him. Yet he'd seemed to remember what his mother said.

It had made James jealous to witness what it was like to have a loving mother. His mother had been a downtrodden drudge who had allowed his father to treat her like an unpaid servant. All James had wanted from life was to read and draw but they took him out of school to help with the farm so often that he could bear it no longer and, at sixteen, he'd run away and joined a group of travellers.

For a few years he was satisfied to travel round the country with them.

However, the longer he stayed with them the more dissatisfied he became. He couldn't get used to the contrast between the way some decorated and cared for their own caravans yet they would rush and cut corners when working for others. He was proud of doing a good job, no matter who it was for. He was grateful that they had accepted him but needed to get away.

His opportunity arose when one of the group stole a number of cans of green paint. Once they had used what they wanted it was time to earn some money with it.

James and a friend were told to look for a likely customer and James was given the task of introducing himself as a decorator and offering to paint the fence.

"It won't work," said James, "unless you let me put a name on the van." They filled it with brushes, a ladder and the left-over paint and James wrote, JIM MANN *painter and decorator* on the sides.

The ruse was successful. James made such a good job of the fence that the owner asked him to paint the outside of the house. The travellers wanted to move on so James paid them for the van, which then became his home – and started life as a decorator.

He wasn't afraid to ask advice in paint shops or look up techniques in the library. Gradually he taught himself more skills.

One day the assistant in the library spoke to him as he replaced a book.

"You must be quite an expert by now."

"What?"

"All these DIY books you read. Your house must be beautiful."

"My house? Are you checking up on me?"

She blushed. "No – I didn't mean to pry."

James looked at her open, smiling face, framed by a deep fringe and long, dark hair. There was something about this girl that intrigued him. She'd not got the fire and fascination of a gypsy or the brazen casualness of the girls he had met in other towns. Here, between London and the coast, he had found a violet among the sunflowers.

"I think you ought to make it up to me for being nosey," he said.

"I'm sorry." She looked down.

"What do you do at lunchtime?"

"I usually eat a sandwich in the park."

"Easy. I'll get myself one and meet you there. What time?"

Her face shone. "Two o'clock."

"Right – first one there bags a bench." He flashed her a grin and left. What had he done? This was unlike any assignation he had made before. This girl was way out of his league. What would she say if she knew he slept in a van?

He went to a café and ordered a coffee. Then he went through to the washroom. Once he was sure his face and hands were clean he inspected his clothes in the mirror. Well, she'd seen him loads of times. She must have thought these were his working clothes. Actually they were almost all his clothes. They would have to do for today but if he made this a habit....

He stared at himself in the glass. What was happening to him? He'd only just noticed the girl and already she'd got under his skin – or, at least, into his future plans. There was something about the way she had looked at him – as if she knew him better than he knew himself. Impossible – but he would soon find out. He'd have more fun at lunch time than he'd had for weeks.

It took six months for James to make enough money to move out of the van, into bed and breakfast accommodation, building up a reputation as a reliable tradesman as he went. His clientele were comfortably off and he learned as much from the way their homes were furnished as he had from the books in the library. None of them seemed to mind that he asked for payment in cash.

Once he felt confident enough, and had built up a reasonable wardrobe, he began to take Anne out. She loved heritage sites and country houses and her eyes lit up when she saw grand staircases or stained glass windows.

"You should have been a princess," he joked, one day.

"Only if you were the prince." She said it so softly he almost didn't hear her.

"Will you marry me, Anne?" The words leaped out of his mouth by themselves.

"Oh. Do you mean that, James?" She looked up into his eyes, searching for the truth. "You aren't just joking?"

It was too soon. He wasn't ready to settle down. He hadn't even met her parents. Why had he said it?

"No – I'm deadly serious. I'd like to whisk you off to a desert island – but I'll be happy if you just say yes."

"Of course I'll say yes. I've loved you from the moment I saw you. You just don't know how special you are."

He hugged her tightly. "I couldn't risk letting you go," he said and knew in an instant that was what had driven him.

And then, when she'd needed him most, he had let her go. In fact he had abandoned her as the fear of having a disabled child had blinded him to everything else. His love for his wife had been swamped by feelings of jealousy and impotence and, once again, he had run away.

All his life he seemed to have been running away – away from tasks he did not want to do, away from form filling and red tape, away from responsibilities and duties. He'd gained his freedom all right – but he had no-one in his life who really cared what happened to him and that he could show he cared about.

114

The museum and the library were shut for the holiday. There was nowhere else he could turn to for help. He would have to park up and wait. There was an empty car park by the beach. It suited his mood, desolate and cold.

Sitting alone, he was assailed by doubts. What if after all this time he was rejected? What if this Ned wasn't his son, James Bernard? What if it was and the boy, now a man, hated him? Only the picture of the long haired little girl in the paper gave him hope. He needed to know if he really did have a granddaughter. If fate had been that kind to him he promised to make it up to them and give her all the love he should have lavished on his son. I'm sorry, Anne, he thought, as he remembered the first years of their romance.

Anne had seemed to sense that James had not planned his proposal and did not try to discuss wedding plans – which was just as well – because, one day, when he met her after work she didn't seem her usual cheerful self.

"What's up, love?" he asked.

"It's my mother. You know I come in on the bus every day. Well, I haven't taken you home because she is very frail and, frankly, I was ashamed of the place. Then, last night, she dropped a kettle on her foot and had to go into hospital. They won't let her out until someone is there to look after her. I'm going to have to give up work."

"Can't you get someone in?"

"No. You see – she's becoming very confused. I've put it off as long as possible – but there's too much she can't do for herself – and she was beginning to wander. The neighbour brought her back from the shops last week and stayed with her until I came home. I felt so guilty."

"Would you like me to run you back?"

"Yes, please. I think she'd better meet you before it's

too late, though I doubt if she'll understand who you are."

"Have you told her about me?"

"Yes – but she doesn't remember. I'm sorry, James – I didn't want to burden you with all this."

"I just want to be with you, you know. It doesn't matter where I am. I can find work anywhere."

"Thank you. Thank you so much."

Once he was there, he stayed. He found lodgings near the beach. It was like being back at Blackpool. Hotels and guest houses welcomed him and he enjoyed walks along the beach and over the Downs.

Anne wouldn't let him redecorate the house. She said it would confuse her mother. There seemed little that did not confuse her. The only time she seemed content was at meal times. The rest of the time she alternated between sleeping and crying out for attention. Anne told him the worst time was at night. Her mother often woke early and wanted to get dressed and go out. It did not seem to matter to her that it was dark and she couldn't see where she wanted to go. Sometimes she wanted to visit friends from long ago – or a shop that had long since closed down. The saddest time was when she called out for her own mother.

James tried his best to help. He sat with the old lady while Anne shopped for essentials and took her list round the supermarket once a week. He made her agree to a carer coming in for two hours a week so that he and Anne could get out of the house together. Then, one morning, his mobile phone rang.

"She's gone." It was Anne's voice.

"What? She's gone off somewhere?"

"No. She had that nasty cough and I called the doctor.

He gave her some pills and she seemed better than she had for days. Then I went to get her up this morning and she...."

"I'll come straight away. Are you OK?"

"Yes. I called the surgery and they're sending someone at lunchtime. I don't know what else to do."

Her voice was wavering and he wanted to get off the phone and get moving.

"Put the kettle on. I'll be there in ten minutes."

They left a six month gap after the funeral before they had the wedding. James invited his brother in Yorkshire but he said he couldn't leave the farm. Anne had a distant cousin and her colleagues from the library. It was a small registry office ceremony followed by a week in an isolated hotel in Wales.

James could hardly believe his luck. Anne was all he could wish for in a companion. Although she had not travelled, she read voraciously and impressed him with her historical knowledge. She was a skilful cook and made left-overs into imaginative feasts. Now that they could do what they liked with the house they had endless discussions about colour schemes and as each room was completed she seemed happier and prouder.

Anne made him feel as if his whole life had been a journey to this destination and when she found part-time work in a local bookshop it became possible for them to begin to save for the future.

"One day we'll have a house with a garage and a workshop and a garden without wire fences that the neighbours can see through."

"But I like talking to Mrs Grant," laughed Anne, "although the children on the other side can get a bit noisy."

They hadn't really discussed children before they were married. James assumed Anne would like a child at some stage but it was something they left to fate – and fate was to test their love to the limit.

Once Anne was pregnant James got used to the idea. He was determined to treat his child better than his father had treated him. James's child would be clever, like his mother. They would spend time with him and encourage him and not use the television as a babysitter. He couldn't help calling it 'him' and when his son was born was delighted to have him christened James Bernard Longman.

Anne had attended the local church ever since she was a child and James was amazed at how many people came to the house to wish them well.

Baby James was an easy baby to care for. He was big and strong and rarely cried. He showed an interest in bright lights and would reach out for anything colourful.

James and Anne bought him picture books that popped up, picture books that squeaked and a picture book with a record, which for some reason was greeted with angry tears.

"It must be because the voices are too American," said Anne. "It doesn't sound like us."

But worse was to come.

They had expected difficulties when he started school. He'd not been used to socialising with other children and, after the half –day introduction, Anne had recognised that her son had obviously been overwhelmed and possibly frightened by the experience.

The teacher took her to one side and asked, "Could you come with him for a week – just to get him used to it?"

The week became a month and James still clung to her and hardly spoke to any other children. Eventually the head called both parents to her office.

"James should be able to manage on his own by now. I know you have a part time job. He's going to have to get used to doing without you. I suggest we introduce a teaching assistant and let you cut down your time gradually until she can take over completely."

So it was that Anne no longer witnessed the difficulties her son had at school and no longer compared him with his peers.

It was a shock to both of them when, at the end of the first year they were told their son had 'special needs.' James was in the middle of a very demanding project, the complete renovation of a big hotel. He was having to cooperate with carpenters and plumbers and make the décor look expensive on a very tight budget. He hardly listened to what was being said at the parents' evening.

Anne was told not to worry about their son – he was probably just a 'late developer' and another year went by without the parents fully realising the extent of his problems.

The boy was almost seven when James found out he could still not read a simple sentence. He copied short lines of writing under those written by a teacher but made no attempt to write anything himself. Yet he would point out pictures from books at home and say, "house" or "pig."

James was worried. He asked the men at work about their children. Then he went up to the school to discuss his son's lack of progress with the head – but he'd picked the wrong week. The school was having an inspection and he only had time for a quick chat with the teacher.

"He's very shy," she told him. "Of course, with his learning difficulties he will always find it hard to keep up with the others."

It wasn't what James wanted to hear. He'd pinned his hopes on a son who would achieve more than he had. Now it looked as though he would need support all his life just to make a living. Instead of being a joy his offspring was to be a burden.

That night he could not sleep. Was it his fault that his son had problems? Was it something in his family, or his life that had caused it? His family weren't academic but they knew how to work and had their own wisdom. None of the men had problems with reading and writing.

Could he have been exposed to anything? He'd heard of soldiers being affected by nuclear fall out or injections. Could the sheep-dip or insecticide on the farm have affected him? If so – he should never have any more children. As if he wanted any!

He was dangerously close to hating the one he had – and beginning to hate Anne for producing him. He knew it wasn't her fault – but he wasn't sure he could go on treating her the way he had always done.

They had been arguing more recently and had booked a holiday in a caravan in the West Country to get away and have a change. He'd meant it to be a way of building bridges but the thought of being with the two of them in an enclosed space for 24 hours a day was beginning to fill him with horror.

He was no longer making his family happy. His dissatisfaction was so obvious he was making them miserable. He thought they could be happy together if he wasn't there and so, half way through the holiday, he'd left – determined never to be found.

Christmas at Lane's End was the happiest Katie had ever known. Having the new dog in the house meant everyone could share in its antics – instead of being divided they all seemed to work together. Of course the adults spoilt Heather and got enormous pleasure out of seeing her open her presents. The place was decorated with a real tree covered in coloured lights and they hung cards round the walls instead of paper chains.

The dog chased balloons until they popped so they hung more high out of her reach.

All Bernard and Katie's old friends from the harbour seemed to have remembered them and they even had a card from Treetops, the day centre that Bernard had attended so many years ago. The whole family went to a carol service at the church and came home to find Sandy had eaten a box of mince pies and been sick all over the kitchen floor.

"It was my fault," said Rose, "I shouldn't have left them out."

"Your home-made ones are better, anyway," laughed Katie.

Pat and George came for Christmas lunch and they all pulled crackers and wore paper hats. This is how Christmas should feel, thought Katie, as she and Bernard sat with Rose in the late evening, relaxing after a hectic day.

Her husband had bought her an eternity ring and she had promised to wear it always. She had given him a cable sweater which he changed into straight away although it must have been too warm.

Bernard's friends from college had sent cards and Lisa had written a long letter which Katie had read out. John had found a similar establishment to the college Bernard had attended in his own county and was beginning there in the New Year.

He had an interview, wrote Lisa, *and they said there was no reason why he couldn't learn to touch-type and get a job .I think he's set his heart on helping people worse off than himself.*

Katie wrote back and told her how difficult it was, not telling Heather about the baby and how they were going to wait until after her birthday. *We are going to take her to the pantomime. This year it's Cinderella. She'll love that.*

James was also looking at Cinderella – but not the pantomime. He had turned up at the infant school on the first day of term and explained that his name was Longman and that he understood that someone with the same name had made a mosaic wall in the school garden. He asked if he could see it and if the headmistress could tell him about the artist. The headmistress was overjoyed and explained why Bernard was called Ned.

"It was a mistake by the old lady. She misheard him when she first asked his name and he was too polite to correct her. It was for the best because he was hiding from Katie's father at the time."

"Katie?"

"Yes – his wife. They are living at Lane's End with her mother. They have a little girl now."

"I know, Heather. I saw her picture in the paper. I think I must be her grandfather."

"But you haven't had any contact since Bernard was a child?"

"No. I left them when Bernard was seven. You'll think I was heartless, I know – but at the time I thought it was for the best."

"Do they really not know where you have been all these years?"

"No – and I'm not sure what reception I'll get."

"I know the family well. I could try to find out for you – or, at least, prepare them. It might be quite a shock if you just turned up out of the blue."

"I wish I knew if I was doing the right thing. Did Bernard seem OK to you? I just can't imagine him married."

"He was fine. He was wonderful with the children. He has a very generous spirit, your son. I'm sure he'll be glad to see you."

James didn't feel so positive but he liked the headmistress' reaction. The wall was a revelation – as was the news that Bernard was now running his own market garden. Could he really have changed that much? Why hadn't James given him more of a chance? He'd never imagined anyone would want to marry someone like him. What kind of a girl could this Katie be?

He knew roughly where Chalk Pit Lane was. He'd been in the King's Head once or twice in the past. Now he had to force himself to wait until the headmistress contacted him again.

"There's a phone call for you, Katie."

"Coming - who is it?"

"Pauline Marshall."

"What can she want? I can't send Heather all that way to school." She held the phone to her ear. "Hi, Pauline."

"How are you, Katie?"

"Fine. How's the school?"

"Just the same. I have been thinking about you all. You know all these programmes about ancestry on TV? Well, I wondered what you would all say if you found out where Ned's father was?"

"Pauline – this sounds suspicious."

"No – please tell me."

"I don't really know. I'd be angry, of course – but Ned might be happy. What are you really saying?"

"Just dropping a pebble in the water. If it's possible to find him I want to be sure of the ramifications."

"For goodness' sake don't do anything yet. If you really think you know where he is I need to speak to Ned. I'll get back to you."

Katie felt hot, then cold. They didn't want any more complications. Everything was fine with the family as it was. She wished Pauline hadn't phoned her, especially when she was being so mysterious.

"What was it?" asked Rose.

"Oh, Mum. I don't know what to do. Pauline thinks she may be able to trace Ned's father. How do you think he'd react?"

"I think he'd be afraid at first – but if the man is eager to make up for leaving him – he'd be thrilled. We need to talk to him before they meet. What's his name? James? I'd be prepared to see him first, if you like."

"Mum, that's a great idea. You are nearer his age and you could work out whether it would be good for Ned. I'll tell Pauline. I think she knows more than she's letting on."

So it was that Rose was sitting in the Harbour Tea Rooms waiting to meet the man who had deserted her son-in-law.

The tall figure had to stoop to enter the café. He

looked drawn and anxious and much too thin, she thought, as his eyes moved over the tables and rested on hers. She smiled and nodded towards the vacant chair.

"Rose?" he asked.

"Yes – and you must be James." She held out her hand and he shook it, not firmly enough. He was nervous, she thought, nervous and feeling guilty. She would have to be especially diplomatic.

"Thank you for seeing me," he began, and she was struck by the colour of his eyes, a bright, light blue. If he wasn't so pale and rangy she might even think him attractive, but what man over fifty still wore a ponytail?

"We haven't told Bernard you are here," she said. "Why did you find us now?"

"It was the picture – in the paper – of the little girl."

"Ah, Heather – on the beach."

"Yes. I never thought he'd have children. Is she…?"

"Normal? Yes – very much so, but Bernard is not so different. In fact he is learning to write and he can memorise words. He's a real godsend to me at the smallholding. You missed so much."

Rose found herself picturing Bernard as a child – trying his best to please his father but being ridiculed and rejected. She'd watched her husband, Tim, reduce Katie to tears with his bullying and realised suddenly how much her daughter and Bernard had in common.

This man was different, of course. He was probably more sympathetic than Tim and had chosen to escape from a situation he could not handle, rather than make his child's life miserable. Maybe he could go some way to redeeming himself. She felt she ought to give him a chance.

James was leaning forward, his eyes wide and pleading; a worried frown across his forehead.

"I can't explain. I couldn't bear to see him every day. It didn't seem to matter to Anne, she was happy to spend every waking moment with him, but it was torture for me."

She didn't want to hear any more excuses. She needed to decide what to do next.

"Where are you staying?"

"I have a campervan. I travel around the country. I'm a decorator."

"So that's why Bernard is so artistic. Did Pauline tell you we have a camping site?"

"No."

"Well. There are two hard standings for caravans. You are welcome to use one while you are here. Perhaps we could pretend you are just a visitor while we find out how Bernard would react. Do you know Stable Lane?"

"I think so."

"Well, I'll tell Pat in the shop to expect you in case I'm not there. Are you still looking for work?"

"Sure."

"The outside of the cottages could do with a lick of paint. Meanwhile, how about a drink?"

"I'm so sorry. What can I get you?"

"They have lovely scones, with a cup of tea, please, James."

"I'll have the same." He pushed his chair back and stumbled to his feet.

He really did look bemused by the whole situation. Rose wondered how he would manage the tray. Perhaps she'd been cruel to let him wait on her but something warned her that she needed to stay in control. Was that a flicker of mischief that she felt? She owed this man nothing and felt loyalty only to Bernard. She wished James no harm but she did not intend to make life too easy for him.

9

" B ernard – Mike's heard from Zak. He's coming to fix up your new computer for you and show you how to use it in April. Can you wait that long?" Chantelle looked up from behind her counter.

"Sure – but I like doing things the way we are."

"I've got a new idea. I've made a card – look."

She brought out a sheet of white card with the title ENDINGS.

"As you read in patterns I thought we'd try this. You know COOK?

"Yes, cook."

"Well – this is COOKING. Say it."

"Cooking."

"Now, if I write some more underneath see if you can tell me what they are."

She wrote LOOKING and PARKING and Bernard found he could read them easily.

"See – all you have to remember is ING and you can

127

make loads of words."

"Swimming?"

"That's a bit tricky – but it's a good start. When you get your computer it will have a spell checker."

"That will be great," he said, unconvincingly, "but I'd better get Heather home. She's with Pat."

"Oh, Bernard. It's pouring with rain. What's she got on her feet?"

"Shoes."

"Well- I've got some new Wellingtons in – look – with pink and yellow flowers. What size is she?"

"I don't know. I'll bring her over. She'll love those."

The fields were getting so muddy they took the long way round up Chalk Pit Lane and shook themselves like dogs as they entered the porch.

"See my new boots, Nana!" Bernard just stopped Heather marching into the kitchen.

"Lovely, darling," Rose replied. "Now get your coat off and come and get dry. Bernard, could you check on the chickens, please?"

"Right. I'll go and shut them in."

That evening, after Heather had gone to bed, Rose at last had the chance to talk to Bernard on his own.

"Bernard, what did your mother do when your father left?"

"She went very sad. I think she cried in her bedroom and she went to church a lot – but she never said anything bad about him."

"And how did you feel?"

"I don't know – a mixture. I missed him. When he wasn't cross with me he was different – sort of by himself. I liked watching him. Seeing John with Ryan made me remember."

"They said they'd come to the camp site in the summer?"

"Yes. Now I'd better get on with Heather's birthday present while she's asleep."

Bernard had meant to make a doll's house for Christmas but when he saw how she had loved to play with Pat he had decided to change it to a shop instead. He kept it in the study and once he had gone Rose began to wonder if James had arrived yet. She would go and see Pat first thing in the morning.

Katie followed her mother into the kitchen after breakfast.

"What happened yesterday?" she asked. "What's he like?"

"He's a bit strange. He looks like an old hippie. He's very thin, not like Bernard, but fair – well, he probably used to be fair, he's grey now, with a ponytail."

"I don't mean what does he look like. What did he say?"

"He was a bit pathetic. He still thinks of Bernard as a boy. He must have been really upset when he found he wasn't intelligent. He couldn't seem to realise what kind of man he'd become."

"Well he didn't wait around to see, did he? I don't understand how he could leave his son AND his wife."

"I think he must have felt a bit pushed out. I don't know. Anyway – I've arranged for him to park his camper on the site. I'll tell Pat who he is but we'll see if we can get to know him better before we tell Bernard."

"I'm not sure I want Heather to meet him."

"It was her picture that brought him here. He'd be proud of her."

"It seems to me all he'll bring her is trouble. A man

like that won't make a very dependable grandfather."

"It's hard – but we should at least let Bernard decide. He's the only family he has left."

"I can't tell him, Mum. He'd sense how I feel. He knows when I'm being negative."

"I'll try to find out how he'd feel. There's no need to rush things. Don't you worry."

James manoeuvred the campervan past the shop, round the end of the toilet block and onto the hard standing. It was a perfect spot to stay, he thought – near the village and the pub and with purpose built facilities. There were no tents now, of course, but he imagined it could get popular later in the year.

When Pat offered him a cup of coffee he accepted gratefully and sat on a stool at the counter. Half an hour later he had a description of the smallholding, he knew all about the units and had learned even more about his son's family.

"I'd like to meet them," he said.

"You will. Bernard will be down in the morning. I'm off now, is there anything you want?"

He bought some fruit and vegetables and took them back to the van. He knew he ought to be out looking for work but he dared not leave. Now he was here all he could think about was being reunited with his son. He felt a mixture of curiosity and fear, as if an unanswered question had lain dormant in his brain and had now grown so large that it had taken over, and nothing else would matter until he found the answer. Most of all, he wanted to somehow prove to himself that he hadn't made things worse by going away, and if Bernard had made a success of his life that would be the proof. However the reunion went, he wanted it to happen soon.

He had a restless night and next morning he couldn't settle in the van so he went out and wandered round to the gift shop. He didn't want to be alone.

The bell rang as he opened the door and a large cheery woman came out from the back room. Looking at her was like looking at sunshine, he thought.

"Can I help you?" she smiled.

"I'm just browsing. I'm parked round the corner for a while and just thought I'd explore."

"There's not much around here, I'm afraid. Are you on your own?"

"Yes." He almost said, "I haven't a family," but stopped himself.

"There's postcards and writing paper," she offered, "and a booklet about the surrounding area."

"Are there any pubs that put on folk music?" he asked hopefully.

"Well, the King's Head doesn't but the pub in the village does, and they have Morris dancers now and again."

"I'll wander along there tonight then, thank you." He paused, waiting for her to supply a name.

"Chantelle," she giggled. "I know it doesn't suit me but it looks good above the shop."

"I'm sorry, I didn't notice – and it does suit you. It sounds like a song and you would lift anyone's spirits."

"Get away – flatterer. Where did you get your gift of the gab?"

He laughed out loud and was still laughing when the door opened and a tall young man entered.

James turned to see who it was and knew immediately

that it had to be Bernard.

He must have been staring because Bernard, who had been about to speak to Chantelle, turned his attention to the newcomer. His forehead wrinkled into a frown. He turned away and then looked back.

James tried to busy himself with the rack of postcards but Bernard had sensed his unease. "Is that your campervan in the campsite?" he asked.

"Yes," muttered James, hoping his voice would not give him away. "Rose said I could stay for a bit."

"It's very nice." Bernard's mouth spoke the words but his face was showing the conflict in his head. "I know you, don't I?" he said at last and James lifted his head.

He looked at the big, open face of his son and watched the puzzlement turn into confusion.

Bernard seemed to be struggling to suppress a thought that was forcing itself to the surface. Was it recognition or revulsion? Had it been just too many years apart?

"You are my father!" he exclaimed at last.

"Yes, Bernie. I'm sorry."

For a second James did not know what Bernard would do and then, with a shout, he was enveloped in his son's burly arms.

"Dad! You're OK. I thought I'd never see you again."

James felt tears come to his eyes. "I'm sorry, I'm so sorry," was all he could say.

"Here, sit down." It was Chantelle. "I'll get another chair. You two need a cup of tea."

"Have you got a whisky?" asked James.

"Certainly not – but I'll put lots of sugar in the tea," and she scurried through to the back.

James took a deep breath. "They tell me this is all yours," he began.

"Not really. It belongs to me and Rose. Dad – you've got to meet Katie and Heather. Heather will be so pleased she's got a grandfather."

"Hold on. Calm down. Can we take this a bit slower? Pat told me about Heather. I'd love to see her. I told Rose I'd stay for a bit."

He hadn't imagined how disturbing meeting his son as a grown man would be. Now he'd done so he needed breathing space before he met Heather and Katie. It was Katie he was nervous about. Surely she would have sympathy with Anne. He still hadn't got used to the idea that his wife was dead.

"I'm sorry you had to deal with everything when you lost your mother." He couldn't bring himself to use the word 'died.'

"I didn't." Bernard sobered up suddenly. "The vicar saw to everything. I wasn't there.

It was only later that we got her ashes. I've kept them, Dad."

James was instantly quiet. A picture of a laughing, happy Anne, young and vibrant, in the days before she had Bernard flashed before his eyes and gave him a sensation of pain in his chest. He shook his head to rid himself of the image.

"When we've had our tea can you come to the van for a while – just so I get used to seeing you again. I still think of you as a little boy."

"And you can tell me how you found us."

James knew he would feel better on his own turf. So far he could hardly believe that this was his son. He spoke slowly but otherwise there was no sign of the problems he used to have. Could he have been wrong about him? Had he overcome his difficulties?

"Did you ever go back to school?" he asked as soon as they were settled in the van.

Bernard blushed. "No- Mum let me stay home – until I started at the Day Centre."

"Did they teach you to read?"

Bernard began to look uncomfortable. His head drooped and he began to thread his fingers together. "I went to college, Dad. I learnt how to be a gardener and I'm getting a computer."

Time had taught James to be more patient and recognising he had begun to upset his son he just smiled and said, "Well done."

"I've got to get back now. Rose will have tea ready." Bernard looked awkward as he made his escape.

James was still worried. He'd cleared the first hurdle but he suspected he still had a few surprises to come.

Rose was stunned. Never before had Bernard come in and gone straight to his study without saying a word. Surely he couldn't have found out about James already? She couldn't believe they would recognise each other after all these years. But then, James' piercing blue eyes were quite distinctive and he did expect to see his son sooner or later. Should she leave him or wait until he ventured out?

She got supper ready and then called him. Heather had been colouring in her drawing book and hadn't noticed her father's strange behaviour.

"I need the table, now, sweetheart," Rose called out. "Tea's nearly ready."

Bernard came out to eat his meal and looked as if he was trying hard to listen to his daughter – but seemed distracted. It was Rose who took her to bed and read her a story.

When she came downstairs Bernard had washed up the dishes and was hovering in the doorway.

"Sit down, Bernard. Now tell me what's happened."

"Did you know the man in the caravan was my father?"

"Yes – but I didn't expect you to meet up so soon."

"What am I going to say to Katie?"

"Ah!" Rose had tried not to anticipate her daughter's reaction. She knew how defensive she could be about her husband. Now she understood what was upsetting Bernard. It wasn't only meeting his father – it was wondering what Katie would say.

"Was I right to tell him where you were?" She needed to know.

"I don't know. It's made me feel funny. I know I'm not how he remembers me. I'm a bit churned up inside."

"Don't worry about it. It will take time to get adjusted. Was he happy to see you?"

"Yes, I think so. He looks so old, Rose."

"He would, after 25 years. Sleep on it, Bernard. We won't tell Katie till tomorrow."

Bernard was awake before Katie, determined to tell her about his father while they were still alone.

As soon as she returned from the bathroom he held out his hand to her, trying to get her to sit next to him on the bed.

"I met my father yesterday," he blurted out.

Her lips tightened. "What happened?" she said at last.

"He kept saying sorry. He was in Chantelle's shop. He wants to meet Heather."

"I bet he does! I bet he'd like to be part of out family set up – now we have a nice happy home. What did you say to him?"

"I don't remember."

"Yes – but you remember when he left you and your mother and never sent any money or told you where he was!"

"That was a long time ago."

"You be careful, Ned. He could hurt you again. Are you sure Heather needs a grandfather like that?"

She jumped up from the bed and slammed the wardrobe door.

"I'm getting dressed," she said. "Think about it."

All the pleasure Bernard had felt at seeing his father had evaporated. He sat brooding over this new complication. Katie was usually right. He should have waited until Rose was with them. She did not seem so set against his father. Was he wrong to trust him? Should he keep him away from Heather? He was afraid to go down to the campsite now in case he met James.

He went downstairs and looked for Katie in the dining room and the kitchen. She was nowhere to be seen.

Rose was washing dishes at the sink.

"Can I watch you training Sandy, this morning?" he asked Rose.

"Of course. Now she doesn't growl at you anymore she might come back to you if you let her off the lead. Heather and Katie have had their breakfast. I'll have a cup of tea with you and then I can show you what Sandy can do."

He watched, amazed, as Rose told the dog to sit and stay, then went indoors out of sight. Sandy waited patiently until Rose emerged and sat still until she was rewarded with a titbit. The Rose walked her round the garden to heel and finally hid a ball and told her to 'seek.' She found it and Rose called Bernard over to play with them.

"There, she accepts you now," she said.

"That's because you let me feed her."

"And because you are quiet and gentle. I wonder how she'd be with James? I think I'll take her down to see Pat and we might find out. Do you want to come?"

"No, I've got work to do in the orchard."

"Right. Here, Sandy." The dog obediently stood by her side. She stroked its head. "Come on, beautiful. We're going for a walk."

James took his bike out of the van and went into town. He'd put his usual advert in the free paper and then go back to the village. He'd really like an indoor job this weather and the sooner he got known as a reliable worker the more jobs he would get.

He'd not been to the pub the previous night so he decided to try it out in the day. Standing by the bar with a pint he drank in the atmosphere. It was an old, dark pub with low beams and yellowing ceilings. There were pictures of sailing ships and huntsmen round the walls as if they had been collected over the years with no discernable theme. He found a seat by the window and waited. A man with his back to James was complaining about the village hall.

"No-one would volunteer to do the toilets. It's no good having a smart hall and grotty lavatories."

"Could I help? I'm a decorator," said James.

The man turned round, surprised at the interruption.

"Only if you work for peanuts."

"How about if I do it for the advertising?"

"You mean, put up a board when you've finished?"

"Yes – and get a free plug in the Parish Magazine."

"Well - if you'd do that you'd better see the church warden. Walter! There's someone here you may like to know."

They told James when the hall was free and promised him he could have at least two uninterrupted days.

"If I can do the preparation work in the evenings that should be all I need," he said. He was a little disappointed that they had chosen the obvious rose pink for the Ladies' but the blue they supplied for the Gents' was more attractive and, after all, the customer was always right!

It was late afternoon before he got back to the camp site and as he passed the shop Rose came through the gate to the field. She had a brown dog on a lead and as soon as it saw him it gave a low growl.

"No – Sandy," said Rose sharply. "I do wish they'd warned me she didn't like men."

James leant the bike against the building and waited.

"I'm sure it can be cured. You bring her to me. Just keep reassuring her."

Rose slowly moved towards him – all the while soothing the dog. "There's nothing to be afraid of. James is a friend." When they were only a pace away she halted and said "Sit."

Sandy sat. Rose took a treat out of her pocket and gave her one. Then she passed one to James. He slowly held out his hand and offered Sandy the treat but she would not take it.

"Early days," he whispered. "Good dog, Sandy," but the dog's ears were back and she looked as if she wanted to get away.

"Bernard and I have told Katie," said Rose, holding

138

firmly to the lead, "but, like the dog, she doesn't trust you."

"That's understandable."

The idea that someone else had found enough reasons to love his son, and even to marry him, made him very uncomfortable. What had Bernard told her about him? he wondered. He tried to concentrate on what Rose was saying.

"Perhaps if I tell her you are going to be extra security at night."

"Good idea." He'd have to show them he could be relied upon.

"I've got a job in the village already." That should prove he meant to stay.

"You'd better tell me another time. I'll have to get back before dark."

"Would you like me to see you home?"

"No, thanks, James – I've got the dog."

After patching up the plaster, mending small leaks and pulling up the old floor tiles, James was ready to start on the painting. He would have an Oxford and Cambridge theme in the Gents', he decided. He would use the pale blue for the walls and ask for a dark royal blue for the paintwork. The Ladies' wasn't so easy. He really didn't like pink but if he teamed it with bright white paint it would, at least, look fresh and clean.

A week later he was delighted to find the vicar had organised a grand opening and invited the local press. It was to be a Wednesday evening, after the toddlers group had used the facilities in the morning.

James hadn't meant to be around but a lock on one of the doors had come loose and he was still fixing it when the first of the mums arrived.

"Hi, you must be Jim, the decorator," said a short, curvaceous blond. "Wow! What a difference."

"I'll be out of your hair in a tick," said James. "Are you coming tonight?"

"No, sorry. No need, now I've seen it. It will be all stuffy big-wigs."

"Oh, I hope not. Anyway, it's all finished." He didn't want to go out through the fire exit and let in all the cold air. He would have to brave the hall and hope he didn't trip over any crawling babies.

"Would you like a cup of tea?" called the vicar's wife from the kitchen as he went past.

"Thanks – if I'm not in the way."

"Not in here, you're not." She turned to greet some new arrivals. "Good morning, Katie, Heather."

It was the girl from the photograph – her long hair tied back in plaits and her green eyes bright and inquisitive. By her side was a slight, delicate young woman, her dark curls highlighted with auburn streaks. She would have been pretty if she hadn't frowned as she focussed on him.

The vicar's wife handed James his tea. "Here you are, Jim," she said, "or is it really James?"

James did not notice the coquettish look in her eye. He was watching Katie's face – her expression turning from curious to defensive.

"James?" she queried. "THE James?"

"Yes. I believe we are related."

"Not to me, you're not," she snapped, shepherding a protesting Heather away. James didn't try to follow. It wasn't the time or the place – but he was secretly pleased that he had at last caught sight of his granddaughter.

In the cottage the phone rang. Bernard answered it. It was Chantelle.

"Bernard – James has invited me to the hall tonight. Are you going?"

"No. Rose was invited but I'm staying here with Heather."

"Could you ask Rose if I could come up to the house after work and go with her?"

"Sure."

It was for the best, he knew. He'd go down to the hall another day and see what his father had done – but, all the same, he was rather sad at being left out of the celebrations.

10

Katie was fuming. She'd tried to be her usual calm and efficient self but she couldn't get out of her mind the fact that Ned's father had returned and seemed to expect everyone to treat him like a prodigal.

She could see that having him around had unsettled Ned – but he and Rose were happy to give him the benefit of the doubt. They had welcomed him and wanted him to be part of the family.

She didn't feel that way. There was something about him, a kind of restless energy, as if he was always looking for something new. She didn't believe he would stay and then Ned would be hurt all over again.

If only she could make him move on soon – before they became too attached to him. Perhaps Sandy was the answer. If she disliked him he might stay away. Wasn't there a way to train a dog to avoid something? Could she find an item of clothing belonging to James and associate it in the dog's mind with something unpleasant?

She didn't know whether she had the time or the patience

– and it would need her to pretend to be friendly enough to visit his van.

She could try. It was the only plan she could think of.

It was raining hard when she arrived home from work. Heather was in bed and Bernard was in the study.

"No walk, tonight, Sandy," she said, as the dog greeted her rapturously. "I'll let you out the front in case Rose is late."

Bernard came through to the dining room. "Rose isn't back yet," he said.

"She's got to take Chantelle home first," began Katie just as the back door opened.

"My, that wind is strong," said Rose, as she came through the porch. "Have you shut the chickens in, Bernard?"

"Yes."

"Good. Then the best we can do is go to bed and let it blow itself out."

"Do you want a drink, mum?"

"No thanks, darling. I had plenty at the party. It went very well but I'll be up all night if I have any more."

It was a disturbed night for all of them. At one time there was the crack and crash of a falling tree; then they heard the flimsy fence they had erected across the garden give way and fly up to the house, smashing and splitting as it hit the walls.

By 4a.m. they were up and checking under the front doors. Water was seeping in over the sill and the wind was as wild as ever. They blocked the gaps as well as they could with newspaper and rags. Thunder and lightening sent the dog shivering under the table but the lights stayed on and Heather did not wake.

It was still raining when daylight came and they stared out of the kitchen window.

Katie tried not to let anyone see how frightened she was. It wasn't so much the water. She knew the house had resisted rain and snow for years. It was the wind. It was howling in the chimneys and shaking the glass in the old window frames.

Her greatest fear was that it would blow so hard that something would smash against the windows and break them. She had a vision of shattered glass and some object, a rock or a large branch, flying through the air and crashing down on top of them.

The only safe room was the lounge. At least there was an extra door between them and the crumbling hillside. How could the chalk hill and the woods have stood for so long and yet be streaming towards them after a few hours rain?

She dared not go upstairs to find more clothes. Instead she took her coat from its peg in the porch and wrapped herself in it to hide her shivering.

Heather shouted out from upstairs and Rose went up to help her get dressed. When they came down, and she saw Katie in her coat she ran to her and clung on.

"Don't go out, Mummy," she sobbed.

"I'm not. I'm just keeping warm. I'm going to pull my woolly hat down over my ears. Look, doesn't Mummy look funny?"

"Yes," The little girl tried to smile. "Can I wear a hat indoors, too?"

"Why not? Or a pretty scarf. There's lots in the porch. I'll bring some in and see which one suits you."

She didn't like being in the porch. Although it was on the sheltered side of the house she could still hear, and feel, the wind whistling round the edges of the back door. She hurried back to her daughter.

Rose had brought out a box of chocolate biscuits. "Let's play a game," she suggested, "and the winner gets a biscuit."

"The shopping game," said Heather delightedly.

"I'll get the alphabet chart from the toy cupboard," said Katie, "Otherwise I'll never remember the order."

Rose began, "I went to the shop and bought an angel."

"Nana – you always say apple."

"Well, today I said angel, and you've got to remember it."

"I went to the shop and bought a angel and a biscuit," said Heather brightly.

"I went to the shop and bought an angel, a biscuit and a carrot," continued Katie.

Meanwhile Bernard was staring through the kitchen window. It looked as if the water, taking the line of least resistance, had swept round the sides of the cottage and then across the fields, leaving a triangle of bushes still erect in the centre.

"The stream will be over Chalk Pit Lane," said Rose, "The only way to get out will be through the orchard."

"I'll see what it's like," said Bernard, putting on his boots and mac.

When he got outside it was worse than he had feared. The low wall he had built to give them a private garden had held but the two gates, one on either side of the house, had been swept away and debris from the woods was piled up against the barrier. He ploughed through the mud to the orchard. The chicken coop had vanished.

Pieces of wood were scattered through the trees and a lone bird was sheltering under the hedge. Many of the trees had lost branches in the deluge and the rain was still beating down.

He picked up the bedraggled chicken and forced his way back to the cottage. He had to step carefully across the river of soil and water that was rushing through the gap. As he did so there was a roar and a large slice of the hillside came sliding down towards him. The mud and bushes hit the foot of the cottage and made it shudder. There would be no using that entrance for a while.

"I've got one chicken," he called out. "The rest have gone. I'll keep it in the porch so Sandy doesn't upset it."

He found a cardboard box and some paper and sat the bird in it. It looked stunned and he didn't hold out much hope for its survival.

The game had been abandoned by the time he joined the others.

"I'm scared, Daddy," said Heather, hanging round his legs.

"Don't worry. You know the story of the three little pigs? Well, our house is made of bricks. No wolf or storm could blow us down."

He saw Katie looking at him gratefully and knew he'd said the right thing.

"I wonder if James is all right?" said Rose. "I think I'll call him."

"Mum – it's only seven o'clock."

"Yes, but no-one could sleep through this."

James had the presence of mind to turn his home and angle it up the hill. The mud from the fields seemed to divide before it reached him, with half going down Chalk Pit Lane and half down Stable Lane. The car park behind the orchard wall was well protected and the shop was undamaged but the units had water almost a foot deep lapping at them. He made sure all the doors of the toilets and showers were closed and went back to hide in the van.

When his phone rang and he heard Rose the first thing he did was ask after the family.

"Don't try to come up here," she warned. "Wait until it stops."

"Let me know if you need help," he replied. "I'm not much use down here."

A gust of wind made the van shudder. He felt fortunate that he had the toilet block on one side of him and the hedge behind him. He just hoped his home would stay upright.

Rose was upstairs when the wind became stronger. From Heather's window it looked as if most of the wood had cascaded into the garden.

The tall trees were still standing on the hill but the thorn bushes, rotten logs and leaf litter had been carried through the fence by the force of the water and deposited against the front of the house. Lighter branches were floating on the still-moving surge that covered the lawn, making it look eerily and frighteningly alive.

A stray branch crashed against the rattling window. Rose ducked, but the glass stayed intact. She took a deep breath. No-one must see how concerned she really was. It was up to her to keep everyone calm. She turned away from the window and started down the stairs.

"I suppose we'd better take all the valuable stuff upstairs," Katie was saying. "Heather, you find your favourite toys, and Daddy and I will bring the arm chairs and the coffee table."

"There's a camping stove in the outhouse," said Bernard. "I'll get it while I can."

Rose went into the kitchen and started putting tins in boxes. "We don't know how long it will be – but if the water does get in we'll be safe upstairs." She filled a box and carried it up to the first floor. Then she coaxed the dog into her bedroom and watched it hide under the bed. The wind was whistling in the chimney and battering the windows. At least they had food and, for a while at least, hot water.

No sooner had she had the thought than the lights went out.

"Don't panic. I've got candles and matches," she called out. "Bernard, put that hen in your bedroom and move Heather's bed into there. The storm doesn't seem so bad in the back of the house."

Rose's phone rang. It was Pat. "Are you OK?" she asked.

"Yes – and you?"

"The boat rocked about a bit and the river is about a foot higher than usual but we're quite safe. Do you need anything?"

"No. Stay where you are. I can't charge the phone up any more. The electricity has gone."

"Nana, I'm cold," cried Heather.

"Right, find some more winter woollies and another pair of socks. Put a scarf round your neck and pretend you are an Eskimo."

"What's an Eskimo?"

"Daddy will tell you – won't you Bernard?"

"Sure. Come and sit up here and I'll draw their home."

Rose was back in the kitchen when she saw a dark shape pass by outside. "It's James," she called out, "Where's he going?"

Katie went to the back door and looked out. "He's breaking Ned's wall," she began, then realising her mistake she amended it to, "No, he's not. He's chopping at the hedge to let the sludge run out into the lane."

"I'll help him," said Bernard and before she could stop him he was out of the door and wading through the mud to where James was attacking the hedge next to the stile.

"This bloody hedge has been here for centuries," he grunted, but once Bernard joined in they soon made a sizeable gap and were pleased to see the mud draining out of the garden and into the stream.

"Now for the other side," said James and the pair gingerly crossed to the orchard. The hedge here was younger and thinner but the mud would not drain away.

"The slope's not steep enough," said James. "We need to dig a trench."

"But then we won't be able to get out."

"Yes, you will – you'll have to come down the fields to the camp site. You wouldn't want to go out into Stable Lane anyway. It's full of rubbish, bits of tree, roof tiles, bikes and dustbins."

"It smells like a compost heap," said Bernard as they dug.

"Yes – it's mostly topsoil but we are beginning to see chalk. It hasn't reached your front windows yet, has it?"

"Not quite. Rose says when it does we must open the

porch door and let it go right through."

"Have you still got a grate?"

"A great what?"

"A fireplace. If we took some of this wood we might be able to dry it out. You could make a fire."

They picked up the driest looking branches and bits of chicken coop and headed back to the cottage. Their outer coating had been useless against the heavy rain and water had soaked down their necks and inside their boots.

Rose took their coats and brought towels, leaving James to take care of himself, but making Bernard sit down so that she could rub his hair dry. Then she got them to move the dining room table and chairs into the lounge. They managed to get a smoky fire going and huddled round it in silence.

"How did the party go?" asked Katie, eventually.

"Not bad," responded James. "I've had two orders because of it and the possibility of work on the new estate."

"There's going to be a lot more work after the storm," said Rose. "It takes months to dry out flood damage."

Heather had been staring at James ever since he arrived. "Why have you got long hair?" she asked at last.

"Because I like it. In fact, it is probably as long as yours," and he undid the band that was securing it.

Long grey locks, flecked with light brown, tumbled around his shoulders.

"You look like Jesus," said Heather and Katie couldn't stifle a snort.

"I don't think Jesus ever had grey hair," he laughed, tying it back. "Yours is much prettier."

"Let's make some sandwiches," said Katie. "Come on, Heather – you can find something to try to tempt the chicken."

"It's Gertie," said her daughter, "And I don't think she likes the box."

Once they had gone into the kitchen James turned to Bernard. "She's about ready for school, isn't she? How old is she now?"

"Four," replied Bernard. "She's starting part-time at Easter."

James saw by his face he was treading on dangerous ground and changed the subject.

"I saw your mosaics in the school garden," he said.

"The children did most of that. There's a ship on the pub at the harbour, too. Eliza and I did that."

"How did you get involved with this Eliza?"

"She took me in when Mum died. Pat and George live in her houseboat now."

"Lunch is served," called out Rose and they all tucked in to cheese sandwiches and apple juice.

Suddenly there was a rash of phone calls. Evergreens were checking on Katie. The police were checking on Rose, and Chantelle was calling to find out the state of the units.

"Under water, I'm afraid," answered James. "I hate to think how much damage has been done to Mike's equipment."

"Should I try to come down?"

"No. Wait till it eases off. There's nothing you can do. There's no electricity and the courtyard is under inches of water." He looked out of the window as he spoke. The rain was definitely more gentle now – and the wind had dropped. Perhaps they were over the worst.

The water had got through to the dining area but the carpet had soaked most of it up. Apparently the mud outside the front doors was too thick to penetrate their defences.

James declined their offer of a sofa-bed and went back to his camper. He crawled into bed for warmth and wondered if he would ever truly be accepted as part of the family.

Bernard confused him. He seemed willing and able, even creative, but often needed simple instructions to be repeated before he responded. There was some mystery about his disabilities. James was determined to find out what it was.

Katie couldn't help crying. She'd stayed brave for Heather and polite for James but now the enormity of what had happened to them had struck home. The front lawn had gone – hidden under broken fence, tree branches and mud. The fields were wrecked – the winter broccoli uprooted and the currant bushes all but destroyed. Her chickens were dead and the orchard was a shambles.

"Thank goodness there weren't any campers," said Rose, trying to cheer her up.

"Look – the garage is still standing. As soon as we get the electricity back we'll be fine." They rolled up the dining room carpet and took the sodden mess out through the porch. Then they washed the floor with disinfectant and added to the barricades in the front hall. Finally they had a supper of soup and cake, using the little oil stove.

Heather was excited to be sleeping in her parents' room.

"Only for a little while," warned Katie. "You're a big girl now."

She could see the view from Heather's room was one of total destruction with no sign of where the garden ended and the woods began. Although the rain had stopped she could not shake off the feeling of disaster. She'd never be able to get away from Lane's End now. All their savings would be spent putting the place to rights.

Even the new houses that had been planned for the other side of Stable Lane would probably not be built if the same thing had happened there. She hadn't realised how much she had pinned her hopes on them.

She'd had a dream that she'd shared with no-one –of a modern house, with a bedroom for each of the children and a modern kitchen with all the latest fitments that she could choose for herself. After all, there was another baby on the way and Lane's End was not the ideal place to bring up an infant. It was going to be rather crowded and if she stayed at home she would have to share the old, narrow kitchen.

The village had fared better than Lane's End. Although it was in a natural valley it was still slightly further up the hill and, rather than entering the houses, the water had turned the lane into a river and run past the orchard towards the sea. The other side of Smallbridge Lane was a flood plain and, once the debris of wood, bricks and rubbish that had rolled down, breaking up the road surface and piling up against the hedges in Stable Lane, had been cleared, that could be made passable.

"It's more like Un-stable Lane," said Pat when she arrived the next day. Amazingly the shop was untouched. There was a step up to the door, which was set on the side so avoided a direct flood. Only the contents of the freezers would have to be disposed of.

Bernard and Mike were busy hauling out all the computer equipment and filing cabinets from the unit.

"Just a pity it was all on one floor," said Mike. "At least the orders in the van are OK. I had them at home."

When Chantelle arrived, James helped her carry the unspoilt stock into his caravan. The electricity had been restored but because the units had taken the full force of the storm there was very little left to save.

"All the cards in the drawers are ruined," moaned Chantelle, "and all the soft toys and cushions. The place smells horrible."

Once they had removed as much as they could, they left Mike sweeping the courtyard and tramped up to Lane's End to try to clear the garden.

They avoided Stable Lane. Bernard had seen for himself what Pat had meant.

The copper beech hedge had survived, but it was covered in debris – plastic bags, paper, a sock, a glove and an upside down umbrella. The road was even worse – mud had banked up the sides and the surface was pitted with holes. Bits of crumbly tarmac were mixed with clods of earth and grass, tin cans, tiles and fencing. It was almost impossible to find space to walk and extremely dangerous for vehicles.

"We'll have a bonfire where the chickens used to be," said Bernard, surveying what was left of their garden.

"Yes, after we've dug all the mud away from the house. Where do you want it, Bernard?" asked James.

It was Rose who replied. "If you pile it against the hedge there'll be no need to go the other side of what's left of the wall," she said. "That will do for now. Then, as the gates are gone, we could take some through to the fields."

So they set to work, Bernard picking up all the trees and branches and making a pile and James shovelling the mud to the side or filling buckets for Chantelle to carry round to the back of the house. They dug a shallow trench round where they thought the garden should be. The chalk was exposed at near the top of the hill and large tree roots were poking through.

"I think that will be your boundary, now, Bernard," said James.

"When it's dried out I'll build another wall."

"Tea and flapjacks," called Rose. "Food for the workers. I've made pork in cider for supper. I hope you're all staying."

"Is Pat coming too?"

"Yes, Chantelle. We need to celebrate that we are all unhurt."

"Where's Katie?" asked Bernard.

"She had a headache. She's gone to lie down."

"She's not doing too much, is she?"

"No, I think she was writing a letter to Lisa."

James stretched upright, easing his back. "I meant to ask you, Rose. Is she expecting another baby?"

"Yes, in June." Rose had replied before she realised Heather was in earshot.

"Are we going to get a baby?" asked the little girl.

"Yes, but not for a long time."

"Why can't we get it now?"

"Because it has to grow."

"Where?"

"In Mummy's tummy."

"Mummy has a baby in her tummy?"

"Yes."

"Where does her dinner go?"

"That is a different part of her tummy. There's plenty of room for both. The baby is in a special part - but you'll have to remember as she gets bigger Mummy will get tired so you mustn't jump about too much. Now, see if you can creep upstairs and bring that stupid dog down. It's time she went out."

"I'll just make myself scarce, then, shall I?" said James.

"No. Just sit still and ignore her. It worked with Bernard and it should with you."

There was a squeaking sound from the hall as the toy they had bought for Sandy bumped down the stairs.

"She'll never learn to be quiet," Rose said, with affection.

"I'll take Sandy to the orchard and see what the damage is," said Bernard. "Then we can pick Pat up on the way back."

The dog was so excited at being taken out she did not seem to notice James. He leant back in his chair and his eyelids drooped. Rose and Chantelle left him to sleep and went into the kitchen.

Katie accompanied her husband to the doctor's surgery.

"I can't see any ear wax," he said, after the examination. "I think there may be a problem in one ear. I'll book an appointment for you to see the audiologist."

"Could he always have had this problem?" asked Katie.

"Possibly – either from birth or due to a childhood illness. They didn't have the tests we do now thirty years ago."

"You'd have thought someone would have noticed."

Katie's anger showed in her voice.

"Don't be cross, Katie. I can still hear you," said Bernard as they left.

"I'm not angry at you. I'm angry at the system and at people who should have known better."

She named no names but, for the first time, wondered what had made Anne keep her son away from the agencies that might have helped him.

"I'm surprised they didn't test you at school," she said.

"I think I was ill. I don't really remember."

Katie wondered if James would have an answer. She doubted it.

When they got back to the cottage Rose was putting things away in the kitchen cupboards in an unusually nervous manner.

"What's happened, Mum?"

"I've had a visitor."

"Oh, yes – who?"

"Some big businessman. He left his card. He wants to buy the smallholding."

"And do what?"

"Put a Garden Centre here."

"Mum, he's just picked you because of the flood."

"I know. I told him I wasn't interested. How could we uproot ourselves now with Heather starting school and the new baby on the way? No – we need to concentrate on getting the place sorted. The hedges need fixing and we need some potatoes in the middle field. I'll decide what to put in the lower one later."

Katie felt confused. Part of her was reassured that her mother was determined to carry on – but part of her was hopeful that eventually they could have a life without the constant effort required to keep the market garden profitable. The thought that someone could actually be willing to buy them out now had given her heart a sudden lift but she concealed it from her mother. She had to agree – this was not the right time.

James was elated. He had been right. Now – once Bernard could hear properly perhaps he'd learn to read and write. Pleased as he was to see what his son had achieved he hated to see him relying so much on women – and not the kind of women James had been used to.

In all the years since he had left Anne he had never found anyone to match her. He'd found ladies to entertain him for a while, widowed ladies who wanted to mother him and, once, a fiery little blonde who teased and taunted him and then left him for a sailor.

If he'd been asked he would have said he didn't like bossy, opinionated, women, but then he wouldn't have been happy with a passive housewife, either. He thought he was content on his own until he met Rose and Heather.

There was a lot about Rose that he admired.

He liked the way she never stopped working, planning, trying to make life better for her family. He loved her cooking, which made his efforts seem tasteless in comparison, and he felt warm and comfortable around her.

It was different with Heather. He was constantly amazed at how bright and energetic she was – always on the move, constantly asking questions. She was just the sort of child he would have wished for.

She made him delighted and resentful at the same time. Why couldn't Bernard have been more like her?

He could feel himself being sucked into their circle, beginning to care what happened to them. Is this what he really wanted, or deserved? Would this be his life for ever?

He thought back to his time, travelling from place to place, alone, but free to do what he liked, when he liked. Could he change and settled down or was there a part of him that was beginning to feel suffocated?

He had still not convinced Katie that he could be trusted, but there was one young woman who seemed to understand him.

He'd talk to Chantelle. He would offer to redecorate her shop as soon as it had dried out.

The thought cheered him. Perhaps the storm had done some good, after all.

The results from Bernard's hearing tests confirmed what the doctor had suspected. One ear had almost no hearing at all, but could feel vibrations, the other was defective, in that it could not hear the full range of sound, but it was near enough normal not to need an aid.

"Can he have a hearing aid for the other ear?" asked Katie.

"I'm afraid not. At his age his brain has got used to only using the one ear. The only advice I can give is to monitor the situation because, as you can imagine, if the hearing in the good ear deteriorates with age we may have to do something."

"I'm sorry, Katie." Bernard looked distressed.

"It isn't your fault. It does explain a lot."

Her husband's problems had always seemed inconsistent but now there was an explanation. No-one could remember something they had never heard in the first place. No wonder he'd had such difficulty at school.

"I don't think you would have liked a hearing aid, anyway," she said. "Let's go home and tell Mum."

Although Rose was glad they had the answer she knew there was someone who would not be content with the diagnosis. She needed to talk to James somewhere other than at Lane's End. She walked down to the shop through the fields. Stable Lane was being resurfaced. They were lucky they were able to use Chalk Pit Lane.

It had only taken Bernard a couple of hours to clear the loose branches from the roadway and the river had quickly gone back to being a water-filled ditch. When she asked Pat about James she said, "He's at the Dog and Duck most weekends. He'll be there this week now they've resurfaced the lane. Sunday nights they let local musicians play in the lounge bar. I hear he's quite popular."

"Why – what does he do?"

"He plays the harmonica – and sings a bit. You should go along."

"On my own?"

"Not necessarily. George will be home this weekend. Come with us. We might not stay all evening but I expect James would see you home."

"I'll think about it. I really wanted to talk to him alone, but he's not in the van and now you've got me intrigued."

11

The little pub was crowded when Pat, George and Rose entered on Sunday night. Immediately they were greeted like long lost friends by a number of customers who used to be regulars at the King's Head.

James was sitting at a table with a group of younger people who, they soon discovered, were also performers. They were treated to blues, skiffle, classical guitar and a rather nervous singer-songwriter, before James rose and played a couple of jigs on his harmonica.

Hardly had the applause died down when he was introducing, "The sweetest voice in the county," and Chantelle got up to sing. As she sang Bunch of Thyme, all chatter in the bar ceased, and when she had finished the applause was so loud she shook her head as if to make people stop.

"Sing another one, Chantelle," came a voice from the crowd. "Sing Chains of Love."

"I haven't rehearsed it," she said, her voice almost a whisper. "I'll do it next week."

She slid into her seat as if trying to hide from the attention.

"Hallo Rose, Pat, George."

"That was beautiful," said George. "Everything James says about you is true."

"Don't take any notice of him," said James. "Can I get anyone a drink?"

"We're fine," responded George, "but I'm sure you can manage another pint. What are you drinking, Chantelle?"

"Just orange juice and lemonade, please, George. Thank you."

It was eleven o'clock before Rose realised that she hadn't had a chance to talk to James on his own. "How did you get here, James?" she asked.

"I walked. I can't ride a bike with a skinful," he laughed.

"Would you like a lift home?"

"Hey, watch out, James, she wants to take advantage of you!" someone called out.

"Got to do what the landlady says," responded James with a grin.

Rose wasn't quite sure she liked being referred to as the landlady, but it was better than having him call her Grandma.

However, listening to the folk in the pub had made her realise how ridiculous the idea of talking sense to James this evening would be. She determined to find a time when she could speak to him in peace, perhaps in the office. She'd need to be in there more now they were getting bookings for the camp site. Easter looked nearly full.

James was humming to himself as they pulled up in the shop car park.

"Here you are, James. Can you manage from here?"

"Certainly, Rose, flower," he replied, and then chuckled at his own joke.

"Get on with you - you're drunk."

"Just merry, pet – just merry," and he stumbled out of the van and across the courtyard to his home.

The night seemed to get darker to Rose. She shivered. She didn't feel like putting the van in the garage tonight. She left it in the lane until morning.

Someone was knocking on the back door. Sandy began to bark. Rose switched on the bedside light. Who would disturb them this time of night? She reached for her watch. It was 1.30 am.

The knocking was more intermittent now – as if the caller had seen the light and realised someone was awake.

She pushed back the sheets and grabbed her dressing gown. Her bare feet found her slippers and she looked round for a weapon. Had someone damaged her car? It did not sound like the police. She could only find a hairbrush but she held it out in front of her as she opened the bedroom door. Katie and Bernard were hovering at the top of the stairs.

"I think there's more than one of them," whispered Katie. "Ned, you go first." The three of them started down the stairs. As soon as they switched on another light the knocking stopped. Katie shut Sandy in the lounge and Bernard opened the porch door.

"Who is it?" he called out.

"Please, it's Jessie. Please help us. Can we come in?"

Bernard looked at Rose who nodded her assent and he opened the door.

Three people stood shivering on the step. Jessie and the twins seemed hesitant to enter until Bernard stood aside and Rose put her arms round the children.

"Who is it?" called Katie from behind Bernard, and Jess's face broke into a watery smile.

"It's me, Katie. I've done it at last. I've left him."

"Come on in. We'll make a hot drink and you can tell us all about it."

Bernard took the small suitcase Jessica was carrying and they all traipsed into the dining room and sat round the table. Josh and Emma looked pale and scared and Jess had a yellow bruise on her cheek and a split lip.

"What happened?" asked Katie when Rose had supplied them all with mugs of hot chocolate.

"They made me redundant from that cleaning job. I couldn't get anything else local.

He's stopped me using the car. Then when I went to the Job Centre I saw an advert for bricklayers. Tony used to be a bricklayer. All the jobs that I could do started before the buses start running. They suggested I retrain but I can't afford to go on a course. I'd love to be a reflexologist but he'd never let me."

She paused to take a sip of her drink.

"I tried to pick the right time to tell him, I really did. I let him have his tea in peace.

I didn't interrupt the news. I even got the kids to bed early. I waited until he put the paper down and suggested a drink. He said he was going to the Dog and Duck for a nightcap and asked why I had a funny look on my face."

Katie couldn't help smiling. Jess's wide-eyed rabbit look was part of her charm.

"I told him, then. I told him I'd looked for jobs but all they suggested were courses.

I said it was a pity I wasn't a bricklayer because they were crying out for them."

"What did he say?"

"He went all red in the face. He said I knew he had a bad back. He said I'd better find a job soon or he'd find one for me. Then he stormed upstairs."

"What did he mean?" asked Bernard.

"I think he mixes with some really shady characters who own a nightclub," responded Katie, "But that's enough for now. Let's get the kids to bed."

"You can have my bedroom," said Rose. "I'll just pop up and change the sheets. There's a Z bed in there. Bernard, can you give me a hand?"

Once they had settled the twins and returned downstairs Jessica began to cry. "Tony said he wanted me to go on the game, Katie," she sobbed. "He said it would bring in more money than any other job and I could use some of it to smarten myself up a bit."

"What did you say?"

"I said there was no way Josh and Emma were having a mother who was a prostitute. I said I didn't believe he had a bad back and I was sick of slaving for him. That's when he hit me."

"Has he done it before?"

"Yes – but only when he was drunk. This time he was sober, and the look of hate on his face was unbelievable. I don't know why I stayed with him for so long."

"What did you do?"

"I was stunned. I'd fallen between two chairs and when I got up he'd gone out. I didn't dare wait. I woke the twins and we packed the case and left."

"What made you choose here?"

"I dared not go to Tania. That's the first place he'll look. I knew there were lots of you here and Bernard is bigger than him. I'm sorry. I didn't know what else to do."

Rose put her arm across Jessica's shoulder. "Well, you go off to bed now, love, and we'll decide in the morning. I don't think your man will bother us and if he did find us Sandy would see him off."

"Where will you sleep?" asked Jess, drying her eyes.

"I'll make up the sofa. Don't worry about me. It's really comfortable. Go on, all of you."

Katie and Jessica followed Bernard up the stairs.

"I'll see you in the morning," whispered Katie as Jessica went in to join the twins.

"Thanks, Katie," she replied.

Rose rinsed the mugs in the sink and sat huddled in a duvet in the lounge. Sandy crept up and lay down at her feet.

"We should get some sleep, Sandy, but I'm wide awake. That young woman should see a doctor and the police but if we get involved I'm afraid for Heather. I wonder if she would spend some time on the houseboat?" She frowned. "No, that won't work. With the twins here she'll want to stay. I wish Jess had considered Katie's condition. Still, she's the one who needs protection." She stared at the ceiling, searching for an answer.

Finally she smiled to herself. "If she leaves the twins with us I think I know where she could go to be safe."

Satisfied that she had a solution she curled up on the settee and closed her eyes against the emerging daylight.

"Rachel, do any of your friends have a spare room?"

Rose had waited until after breakfast to make the call. Heather had been delighted to see the twins and they were setting up a tent in the front garden and playing cowboys and Indians.

Jess was hunched in a chair in the lounge – pretending to read the local paper. Bernard had gone down to the camp site and Katie was watching the children.

"Sure, why?"

"One of Katie's friends was bullied by her husband and she's run away. She has two children with her and she needs somewhere to stay."

"Well, there's no room here – better with Frank at the farm. That way there'd be someone around all the time."

"She hasn't got transport."

"She'll just have to learn. Ask her if she can ride a pushbike. If she can do that - riding a motorbike will be a doddle. Frank and June will enjoy teaching her."

"I will. I'll get back to you. Thanks Rachel."

She had a sudden image of Jessica in black leathers with her face obscured by a shiny helmet. She was still smiling when she went to tell Jessica.

"Jess – I've been thinking. The twins are fine here for now but you need to get away. Are you sure you don't want to go to the police?"

"No. I couldn't do that. I just need to be safe."

"I think I've found just the place. There's a farm where the motorbike boys hang out. They've offered to put you up. I'm sure they'll find plenty for you to do. Would you like me to arrange it?"

"Josh and Emma would like to be on a farm. They won't be able to go back to the village school or Tony would find us. We need to be well away from here by the summer."

"Can you ride a bike, Jess?"

"Yes, why?"

"Rachel, the girl who suggested the farm, asked. They'll probably try to get you to join their mob."

"What – ride a motorbike?"

"Yes."

"I'd love to." Her frown broke into a grin. "Oh, if only I could. I'd feel a different person, but they are so heavy." She began to laugh. "Just imagine what Tony would say if I turned up on a motorbike!"

Rose did not want to think of Tony. She tried to get back to practicalities.

"There'd be more job opportunities if you had your own transport."

"Rose, you've made me feel so much better. I must go and tell Katie. She'll never believe it." She jumped up and headed for the garden.

Next day Katie's phone rang. It was Tania. "Katie – did you know that Jessica had run away?"

Katie thought quickly. She didn't want to lie – but she didn't want to give the game away either. "Really? What happened?"

"Tony came back from the pub and found she and the twins had left. He came barging round to us at two in the morning wanting to know where she was."

"Did you know?"

"No. When we told him, and asked if he knew why she had gone, he just collapsed. He seemed to deflate – just like balloon. I've never seen a man change so quickly. One minute he was full of bluster and the next all the fight seemed to drain out of him.

168

He leant on Duane as if they were bosom buddies and then sank into the big chair. He was wailing that he didn't know how to manage without Jess; that he hadn't meant to hurt her; that he was scared of going to prison, all sorts. It all tumbled out in a long stream. I left Duane to it. I couldn't take any more. He must have given him a blanket and settled him down because the next thing I knew Duane was waking me up, saying he was off to work, Tony was asleep, and I was to put painkillers in his tea to keep him calm and ring if he was a problem."

"You poor thing. What did you do?"

"I gave Oliver his breakfast and walked him round to Sally's. By the time I got back Tony had disappeared. I hoped he'd gone home. I didn't know what mood he'd be in. I think we'll get a dog. I'd feel a lot safer."

"It's not you he's mad at, it's Jess."

"You used the right word there, Katie. I think he is a little bit mad. I don't know how she put up with him for so long. He's so unpredictable."

"Well, I'll keep an eye out. Good luck." She rang off before she said too much. For the sake of everyone at Lane's End she had to keep the secret.

Ten days later a trio of motorbikes roared up to the back gate. Katie went out to greet them.

"Hi, Katie," said Jessica, taking off her helmet and shaking out her long hair.

"What do you think?"

"You look great," replied Katie. "It really suits you."

"Oh, Katie. They've been so good to me. Are the twins ready? It's fabulous. They are going to have to share my room but it's enormous. There are bunks on one side and a bed for me on the other and a massive living area with a separate shower and toilet. We have to share the kitchen but I don't mind. We couldn't ask for more. And I've got a job. There's a business park just along the lane from the farm and because it is so out of the way they can't get cleaners."

"Stop, stop. You're going too fast. Come inside and tell us all about it."

Jessica waved at her companions. "I won't be long," she said.

Following Katie along the path to the cottage it seemed she could not stop talking.

"Greg said as I had the contract for five of the eight units I ought to set up my own firm. He suggested I call it, *'Rise and Shine,'* but I think that's a bit suggestive, don't you?"

Katie could hardly believe the change in Jessica. The timid mouse of a friend who had seemed cowed by life was bright-eyed and full of energy.

When they were reunited the twins seemed mesmerised – as if they didn't recognise their new mother. Katie hoped the move would give them the same boost that it had given Jessica.

They piled into the large sidecar connected to one of the other bikes. Heather came to the gate to wave goodbye. Katie put her arm round her daughter. "We'll go and see them when they are settled in." she said, comfortingly, "and you'll be able to meet all the other animals."

She felt old and fat and tired. What would she give for a change of scene, a dash of excitement – something to stop her feeling like a big, useless, suet pudding? There was still over a month before the baby was due and all she could do was wait.

It was Heather's first day at the village school. They had prepared her as well as possible and two of her playmates from toddler group were joining in the same week.

Heather's starting day was a Wednesday. Kate had bought her the two regulation polo shirts, one yellow, and one blue, with the school crest on the pocket – and two little grey skirts. There was also a blue school sweatshirt for cold weather, but no other uniform.

Her daughter clung to her hand in the playground but seemed calmer when they got inside.

"Hallo, Heather. I'm Miss Green – like the colour – there's a locker here with your name on it. Put your coat in there and come and see what you'd like to play with."

They entered the classroom together.

"Do you know anyone here?" asked the teacher.

Heather looked round the room. "Karen," she said.

"Good. Karen, can you show Heather the Wendy House? There's an overall hanging up by the colouring table if you want to paint or draw."

Heather trotted off with her friend without a word to Katie.

"Well I never!" she exclaimed.

"That's normal with the children from the toddler club. They don't realise you aren't staying. It's the ones who have been at home with mum until now who cause all the problems – although I think the mums sometimes get more upset than the children. If you don't want to hang around just tell her quietly you'll be back at lunchtime. She'll be fine."

"She didn't even blink," Katie told Bernard and Rose when she got back to the cottage. "It's a nice day, Ned. Would you like to collect her at twelve? Then I won't have to rush about before work."

Bernard did not like to say no – although the very thought of going into a school made him nervous. Still, he'd be the first to find out how Heather had coped.

She couldn't hide her feelings from him. He'd be able to tell if she was happy or overwhelmed.

The parents waited in the playground and the teacher checked that each child was met by an adult before they dismissed them. Heather ran over to Bernard, her coat loose and waving in the wind.

"Look, Daddy, I drawed Sandy and teacher put her name underneath."

Bernard looked at the picture. Sure enough, the dog was recognisable but although he knew the S the rest of the word was unfamiliar. He tried to smile.

In his eagerness to learn to write he had forgotten that Heather would be taught with the little letters that had caused him so much confusion. He knew how to write the word SAND but this looked nothing like that. What was he going to do? He needed to talk to Zak.

Heather was skipping along the road next to him and chattering about her day. He could hear the sounds she made but it was too quick and far away for him to comprehend. Did it matter? She would say it all again when she saw Katie and Rose.

"What are the flowers in the apple trees, Daddy?" They had reached the orchard.

"That's called blossom. The more blossom we get, the more apples there will be, as long as the bees come."

"Why do you want the bees to come?"

"Because they help turn the flowers into fruit."

"How?"

Bernard realised he had started a conversation he could not finish. "Ask Nana – she's better at explaining."

As if on cue Rose and Sandy came out to greet them.

"Sandy!" Heather called out. "Daddy's got your picture."

Bernard held out the paper and Rose took it. "That's lovely, darling. We'll stick it up in the kitchen where everyone can see it."

Bernard hung back as they went inside. "I'll just check on the new birds," he explained. The replacement chicken coop had five new hens but they didn't seem to like Gertie. The poor thing had been pecked again and had lost a lot more feathers. He would have to separate them somehow.

Straight after tea he phoned Zak and told him about Heather's first day at school.

"I couldn't read the word," he complained. "I'm useless, Zak."

"No – it's my fault. It's taken too long to get that computer. Is Mike back in the shop?"

"Yes – but he hasn't got much stock. He's concentrating on repairs."

"I'll phone him. Meanwhile see if Chantelle can find out more about the system they use to teach reading at the school. It's probably phonics, which won't suit you at all – but it's still time you learnt the small letters. I'll come down at the end of the month.

Don't worry about it, Bernard."

But Bernard did worry. Even when Chantelle showed him how a little "a" looked like an apple and a little "o" was the same as a big O he was still afraid that Heather would learn more quickly than he would. He didn't dare show an interest in her work and he hesitated to tell her stories in case she realised he wasn't reading them.

When she brought home her first reading book he left it to Rose to help her through it.

"She's very quick," he heard Rose telling Katie one evening, "Even when I hid the pictures she knew most of the words."

"She's probably memorising them like Ned does," responded Katie.

"Oh no, when she can't remember them she's sounding them out."

Bernard couldn't bear to hear any more. "I'm going out," he said.

"But it's dark, Ned," said Katie.

"I won't be long. I'll take the dog."

The two women exchanged glances. Now James was at the campsite there was no need for Bernard to patrol – but it wouldn't do any harm. There were three tents in the field and now Sandy was used to Bernard it gave her an extra walk.

"I'm tired, Mum –I'm off to bed," Katie said. "I'm glad I'm finishing work."

"I don't suppose you want a party for your anniversary and Bernard's birthday?"

"Sorry, Mum – not this year. Let's just have a family meal, shall we?"

"James suggested we have a barbeque. Could you manage that?"

"As long as I don't have to go anywhere and don't invite lots of people. I'm just not up to it, Mum - night."

Katie lay in bed waiting for her husband to come home. She wasn't sleeping well these days. She was tired of being pregnant, tired of not being able to manage her own life, and tired of having to share Ned with so many people.

It was James who had unbalanced their lives. She had gone to see him in his van but her plans to get rid of him had faltered when she found he knew so much about the new houses.

Instead of chasing him away she decided to use his knowledge to discover whether the new estate could provide her family with a home. But it was all taking so long and the baby was due soon. Then she would have something else to worry about.

12

Rose sat alone in the lounge, trying to imagine what it would be like with a baby in the house. There was room in the porch for a small pram. It seemed nobody used old fashioned nappies any more so at least the place would not be full of washing all the time. The crib would be in Bernard and Katie's bedroom for at least a year – but then what?

It really might be a good idea to consider selling up- but where would they go? She couldn't envisage living on her own now she had got so used to them being with her.

She was afraid there might come a time when she could become a burden. There again, there was a part of her that would like to travel – but she knew she would not like to do it by herself. Perhaps she should be like James and get herself a little mobile home.

Her thoughts were interrupted by the return of her son-in-law.

"Everything all right, Bernard?"

"Yes. It's all quiet."

She watched him pat the dog and make sure she had some water and then followed him as he trudged up the stairs.

Katie was visiting James in his camper. He had sheets of plans spread out on the table.

"Brian Sampson says they'll be finished by Christmas," James was saying. "The show house is ready for me to decorate and they've started on the terraces."

"So there's two lots of terraced houses fronting the lane and the rest are semi-detached, built round a square?"

"Yes, but one side of the square, the side next to the woods – is open plan garaging. If they'd put houses there the gardens would have been north facing."

"So the houses haven't got their own garages?"

"Well, four of them have – but not the rest. It wasn't supposed to be an expensive site."

"And they're calling it The Meadows not Stable Lane?"

"Yes, all sixteen houses. The best ones would be the two that look out between the terraces."

"How many bedrooms?"

"That's the good part. They have four bedrooms each."

"Do you know what the price will be?"

"Over £250 thousand– but you'll get much more than that from the Garden Centre people."

"It wouldn't be my money, James. It would be my mother's."

"Really? I thought Rose and Bernard were partners?"

Katie opened her mouth to speak and then closed it again. Of course – when her mother arranged the partnership she also made sure that half the house was in their name. They owned half the property and half the land as well as half the business! If it was all sold there might be enough for her and Ned to buy one of the new houses. Their new baby could live in a brand new house. She felt a sudden lightness, as if, instead of carrying a sack of problems, she was holding a balloon of possibilities.

"If she's a girl I might even call her '*Hope*' she giggled. "Thanks, James."

Bernard could not understand it. He thought Zak had come to see him but he'd been closeted in the study with Rose for at least two hours. It was time to collect Heather and he would have to go on his own.

When he reached the school the mothers were milling about and he couldn't see his daughter. Then he noticed the teacher beckoning him over.

"Good afternoon, Mr Longman," she said, "Heather is almost ready."

"I've got a star, Daddy," came a voice from the corridor. Heather was trying to open her school bag while it was still over one shoulder.

"Wait a bit," said Bernard. "Give the bag to me, then you can find what you want."

The book she brought out had lines drawn across each page with a space for a picture above them. Under a picture of a house Heather had written, This is my house.

To Bernard the picture was surprisingly skilful for a young child and he could at least have a good guess at the words underneath.

"Can you read it to me?" he asked.

"This is my home," said Heather.

"Lovely, very good – and I like the star."

They walked back along Stable Lane. The new houses

being built on the field depressed Bernard. He knew people had to have somewhere to live but he remembered the path up through the woods. They wouldn't be able to go that way any more.

He'd enjoyed seeing the expanse of tall grasses as he came out of the orchard and now all he could see was a row of brick houses. He supposed they were quite nice. They had tiny front yards and long back gardens with a flint wall dividing the end properties from the wide driveway into the central area.

He turned away from the lane and through the gate to the orchard. There weren't going to be as many apples as usual. The storm had damaged the trees. Potatoes and onions alone would not bring in as much money as last year. Perhaps it was time he looked for some gardening work?

It was still a surprise to him when, once Heather had gone to bed, Rose told him what she and Zak had been discussing.

"I'm going to get the place valued," she said. "There's no need to worry. It doesn't mean I'm selling up. It's just so I can plan what to do next."

"What did Zak say?"

"He's worried because Mike is giving up his unit – and he's talked to Pat. The shop isn't doing too well, either."

"But there's more campers coming."

"Yes, but the villagers don't use it. Once September is over it might as well not be there."

"What about the new houses?"

"I don't think anyone will move in there until next Spring. Having the shop there was always a risk, but he has an idea he's going to try out. He won't tell me what it is, but he says it's to do with the Garden Centre. He's coming back tomorrow."

The next day Zak arrived carrying a small box. When Bernard went out to help him he said, "It's OK. I can manage this. There's another one in the back. Could you fetch that, please?"

With both boxes on the dining room table Zak looked eagerly at Bernard.

"I've just been to see Mike. We've got you a birthday present. Open it."

Bernard opened the larger box first. It contained a plastic object and some electric cable.

"It's a printer!" gasped Rose, watching from the doorway.

"Yes – and the other box has a lap top. It's not a new one so it won't connect to the internet but it will do to practice on. Things are changing so fast and getting so complicated that this was the best thing to learn on."

Bernard lifted the lid of the computer. There before him were rows of letters – not in the order of the alphabet – but familiar, capital letters.

"Come on, said Rose, "Let's try it out."

Bernard wasn't sure he wanted Rose to watch him but he let Zak take it to the study and plug it in and begin to show them how to open the programs.

"Bernard – you will want Word," he said. "Now, press down on a letter and see what comes up on the screen."

Bernard obediently pressed B and there in front of him was a small b.

"It's gone wrong," he said, looking questioningly at Zak.

"No – it's fine. I forgot you'd want the Caps Lock." Zak pressed a key at the side.

"Now try again."

Bernard pressed B again and the letter B appeared.

"You'll have to learn how to make spaces and how to

make the letters bigger but as long as you press Caps Lock first it will always write the way you know. Later on, when you are used to it we can show you what your words look like in small letters but don't panic – we don't have to do anything in a hurry."

"I'll leave you to it," said Rose.

Bernard stared at the screen as if it had magic powers.

"I'd rather write things down," he muttered.

"You won't learn everything at once but the printer will print everything you write. How about trying a simple sentence? Try My name is Bernard Longman."

"I don't know what 'My' looks like."

"What's the first letter?"

Bernard put his lips together. "M".

"Good. Then you add a "Y".

Bernard typed MY.

"Now, do you remember name?"

Bernard pulled a piece of paper towards him and wrote NAME.

"Fine – now type it".

He took longer, this time, finding the letters, but the word NAME came up on the screen. Unfortunately they hadn't left a space between the two words. Zak leant over and corrected the spacing and then watched while Bernard wrote IS on the paper and then transferred it to the laptop. He then wrote his name and copied it, with only one error when he hit the wrong key, onto the screen.

His forehead was beaded with sweat, his hands slipping on the keys and his face a permanent frown. He sat back at the end of the exercise breathing heavily and near to tears.

"I can't do it, Zak. It's too hard."

"You can. You did."

"But I have to write it first."

"I can see that. I didn't expect it but it makes sense. You see words as one shape, not single letters, but you've got loads of them in your word book. You won't need to write those. You can have that next to you when you use the computer."

Bernard hugged himself as if his body was cooling.

"Can we stop now?" he asked.

"Of course. I'll just show you how to close it and I'll write it all down for Rose."

Relieved, Bernard returned to the dining room. Something Zak had intended as a happy surprise had made him feel shaky and afraid. He would try to understand it while his friend was here – but he doubted if he would use his present once Zak had gone.

Rose separated out the portion of casserole and cut a generous slice of apple pie.

However good a man's cooking was, she thought – he'd always appreciate something extra. She had a suspicion that James lived on microwave meals and was genuinely grateful when she took him some of her home-made fare.

It was finding times when she was able to visit James in his van that was difficult. There always seemed to be someone around and she couldn't always say she was seeing Pat.

James had been helping Chantelle in her shop so he was never far from the camper.

She knocked gently on the door, hoping he was in.

"Just a minute," he called. Then, opening the door, "Come in, Rose. Would you like a coffee?"

"Yes, thank you, James. I just brought some bits and

pieces. I always make too much." She blushed.

"Well sit yourself down. I'll take that. You really shouldn't, Rose – but I won't say no."

"Have you finished smartening up the shop?"

"The gift shop? Yes. It's all fresh and bright – but it will take some time to get back to normal."

"Still, Chantelle still has the mail orders, doesn't she?"

"Yes – and I've drawn some local scenes that we are going to put on the next batch of offers. Would you like to see them?"

"Yes, please."

James brought out a large sketch book and opened it at the first page. There before her was Lane's End, before the flood and without the extra walls. It looked just as she would always remember it, old and beautiful.

"Oh, James – you've captured it perfectly – and in autumn, too. The colours are wonderful."

"It's only pastels. The colours will need to be stronger for printing. I'm not sure that is commercial - but how about this?"

He turned the page. This time the view was of the sea. White waves lashed smooth grey rocks and the blue sky was flecked with gold.

"You really are an artist, aren't you?" she asked, looking up at him.

"Perhaps. But there's no money in it. I've not progressed to canvas. Still – it will be nice if they can be turned into greeting cards."

"You've got hidden depths – haven't you, James?"

"Not, I suspect, hidden from you, Rose. You really understand people, don't you?"

"I try to." She searched his face – hoping he was being sincere.

He reached for her hand and covered it with his. The gesture seemed so perfect she had to swallow hard.

"Thanks for everything, Rose."

His smile lit up his face. She could almost imagine him thirty years ago, young, slim and charming. If only she had met him then. Now it was too late, too late to go travelling to all those places she had never visited and probably too late to let another man into her life.

The moment passed. She finished her coffee and made her exit. The meeting had given her too much to think about. She had become so used to putting other people first that she had almost forgotten to consider her own future. What did she want from the rest of her life?

It was Bernard's birthday. Katie had the day off. She was glad because it was becoming difficult to fit behind the steering wheel when she drove to work.

The party had been a partial success.

George had buttonholed Ned and talked about fruit trees all afternoon. Pat had wanted to know all her preparations for the baby and James and her mother had been competing to remember old folk songs. She had watched them laughing together. Was her mother getting too close to James? He didn't seem to mind.

She'd tried to stay good humoured but she didn't enjoy barbeque food and after one sausage in a bun and a fruit squash she had pleaded that it was too hot outside and retired to the dining room. Heather followed her in.

"Will you read to me, Mummy?" she asked.

"OK. Fetch a book."

Heather brought the story of the three little pigs and Katie carefully read the words, her finger tracing the lines.

"I'll huff, and I'll puff, and I'll blow your house down," joined in Heather, delightedly.

"But our house stayed up," said Katie, dreamily. "They knew how to build houses in those days."

"Another story, Mummy?"

"Not tonight, darling. It's sleeps time now. Show Mummy what a big girl you are and get ready for bed."

Next morning Katie had the house to herself. She sat downstairs musing. There were so many changes coming – no-one seemed to be acting the same – even her mother appeared to be getting sweet on James. The thought disgusted her. In spite of how she had felt about Tim it did not seem right for Rose to get involved with Ned's father. They had all been making James a bit too comfortable – and now he'd found Ned some work at the building site he seemed to think he was truly part of the family.

Ned was to design and structure the garden of the show house. He was so thrilled about it that nothing else seemed to matter. He was going to put forsythia up the fence that backed onto Smallbridge Lane and make half the garden patio and half lawn. He wanted hebes along one side and evergreens along the other. Rose had taken him to the nursery to choose plants and the digger was booked for the following week.

The phone rang and she picked it up.

"It's Barton's – the estate agents. I'm sorry to ask at such short notice but can we change tomorrow's appointment to 3pm?"

"What appointment?"

"Is that Mrs Rose Smith?"

"No – it's her daughter. I think you've made a mistake."

"Mrs Smith asked us to value the property. Is she there?"

Katie was dumbfounded. Why did her mother want to know what Lane's End was worth now? Was she really thinking of selling up and moving? Had James put her up to this?

"Well, she's out at present but I'll give her your message. Thank you."

What should she do? She needed to talk to someone straight away. Who would know what her mother was planning? There was only one person she would confide in – Pat!

She hurried down to the shop and burst inside. Pat was serving a customer and she fidgeted in the background until they had left.

"Pat – what's my mother up to?"

"She hasn't told you?"

"No. The valuers called. She's not going to sell up, is she?"

"Not for a while. There's no need to panic. She's just planning ahead."

"Why didn't she tell me?"

"Because of the baby. She didn't want you upset when all she was doing was 'testing the water' as she put it.

"She wants to know how much the whole place is worth?"

"Yes. Zak is making enquiries about planning permission. She thinks she might let the garden centre people have it."

"But where would she live?"

"That's the sticky part. She is hoping to get permission to turn this place into a residence."

"What would you do, then?"

"I'd try for a job at the Garden Centre. I don't know. I don't really want to retire. It's all too vague at the moment."

"I see."

The seed of hope that had been sown inside Katie began to grow into a tiny shoot. Her mother's plan was helping her dream come true. She let out a sigh. Could it be that, at last, she could have a home of her own? She, Ned and the new baby could stay near to her mother and all their friends and yet be independent, without the worry of having to make the market garden pay. The vision was too bright – it all seemed too easy. She didn't trust that fate would be so kind.

Yet it made her feel good. She felt happier about the baby – happier about Ned – happier about everything. "Oh, Pat. I do hope it works out," was all she dared say.

"Now, don't you go rushing about any more – slow down."

"I will. I'll rest this afternoon. You wait till I see Mum!"

"I can give you two quotes if you like, Mrs Smith – one for the house on its own and one for the whole property."

"I don't want to sell the shop or units or the camp site."

"Well, I can tell you straight away you'd be best advised to go to auction."

"No. I don't want to do that. I want some control over who we sell to."

"Mrs Smith – once it's gone, it's gone. You won't have any say in the matter."

"I know – but I can't help it. It has been in my family for generations."

"Make sure you get good advice – it's a big step."

Didn't she know that? Wasn't she trying to please so many people her head was swimming? She needed to see James. Being with him always made her feel less like a businesswoman and more like a companion.

She liked the way he seemed to treat every problem as an opportunity, even if his solutions did not always chime with hers.

The valuer promised to send her his estimates. He'd been impressed with the ceramic sink but scathing about the way the two cottages had been knocked together. Somehow, just listening to him made her feel less affection for the place. Perhaps it was because she knew whoever bought it was not going to live in it. If it went to the garden centre people they were certain to knock it down.

She went into the porch for her coat.

"Don't go out, Mum. I think something's happening."

Katie had been waiting in the lounge and now stood in the doorway holding her stomach.

"Do you want to go to bed?"

"I'm not sure. Just stay with me, Mum. The bag's packed."

"I know. We've done all we can to prepare. It's up to you, now. Where's Bernard?"

"He's taken Sandy and Heather to see the new houses. They're really smart, mum."

Rose watched as she gulped for air and seemed to find it hard to focus on what her mother was saying.

"I just hope they still have the orchard to look over when they are finished."

"Why?"

"Well. I wasn't going to tell you until after the baby but you met the valuer. I'm thinking of letting someone else have the property. It's only an idea. Nothing is fixed in stone and I wouldn't do it without consulting you and Bernard."

"I've heard that before. When were you going to tell us?"

"When I knew how well the crops had done this year. Now, are you comfortable?"

"No. I want to walk about. I hope Heather doesn't see me like this." She gave a grimace as the pain hit her.

"I'll ring Chantelle. If she can stay for a while she can let Heather play in her shop – and I'll tell Pat. She can come and stay with Bernard when they come home."

"Ahh – mum – I'm making a mess."

"Get into the kitchen. It's easier to mop up there. I'll ring the hospital and tell them we are coming in."

Katie gripped her mother tightly as she bent over the sink.

"I'm scared, Mum. What if something goes wrong? I wish Ned was here."

"Come on. You've done it before. It's always quicker the second time."

"That's what I'm afraid of. What if we don't get there in time?"

"We will. Trust me. Just breathe."

"Look, Chantelle – we've been picking flowers."

Heather waved a drooping bunch of wild flowers at Chantelle as she came out to meet them.

"Lovely. Come into the shop and I'll find a nice vase for them."

"Can we play a game?"

"Yes, of course. Come on, Daddy."

Bernard laughed. It always sounded funny when Chantelle called him that. He was surprised she hadn't closed the shop. Wasn't it about time she went home?

Once they were inside and Heather was busy choosing a game Chantelle told him about Rose's phone call. "Rose is taking her to hospital. She said we were to try and amuse Heather until Pat can take over."

"Can we play Snakes and Ladders?" interrupted Heather.

"That's great – and here comes Granddad. Now we'll have four to play."

"I was coming to walk you home," said James to Chantelle, "but if we're all having fun then I'll stay until you are ready."

"The baby's on the way," whispered Chantelle, then, "A lollipop for the winner."

Bernard turned his attention to the board game. How could he sit here playing while Katie was going to hospital? What if something went wrong? He should be there, with her. Heather would be fine without him.

"Your turn, Bernard," said James.

Bernard fought the mist in his head. He must do what he had been asked to do and trust that everything would be fine. He crossed his fingers and made a silent wish.

'Please keep Katie safe and make her happy."

Neither Bernard nor Pat could bear to put Heather to bed and she was asleep on the sofa when Pat took the call.

"It's a boy," she squealed. "Mother and baby are fine."

"When can we see them?" asked Bernard.

"Tomorrow – in the afternoon. They want to keep them in for a couple of days."

"Is Rose coming back?"

"Yes – but she said don't wait up. I'd better wake Heather. Come on, sweetheart – time for bed."

"Is Mummy home?"

"No – she's in bed at the hospital but she's fine and you have a new baby brother."

"Oh good," Heather said sleepily and snuggled into her father's shoulder as he carried her up the stairs.

He stood looking at her for a while, curled up, holding her fluffy rabbit.

It seemed such a long time ago that she was their baby.

He thought back to the time when they all went on holiday to the college lodge and sat on the hill by the ruins, staring out over the countryside.

Life seemed simpler then. Now events seemed to sweep them along too quickly for him to appreciate all he had. Although he was looking forward to having a son he was wary of more changes. James had resurrected much of the self doubt that he had buried in the successful running of the market garden. He had enjoyed being the man of the household but when his father was around he felt diminished, somehow.

He prayed that he could be a good example to the new baby. He wished Katie was home.

He returned to the lounge to find Pat holding two empty glasses and a bottle of whisky. "Have a drink with me, Bernard, to celebrate?"

"Can I have a sherry, please, Pat? I don't like whisky."

"Of course. You sit down. I'll get the biscuit tin."

Bernard sat down.

He felt dazed – and in the wrong place. He didn't

want to be here with Pat. He should be at the hospital with Katie. When Katie wasn't with him he felt uncertain, happy with what was familiar but nervous about anything unexpected.

A boy! That was unexpected. For some reason they had all thought the baby would be another girl. He was pleased, but he wanted to see that Katie was happy, too.

He sipped his drink. Pat was saying something but he couldn't make out what it was. Still, she looked content. He would finish his drink and go to bed.

13

Bernard spent a restless night and was glad when it was daylight and he could take Sandy for a long walk. How could he wait until the afternoon? He wanted to see for himself that his wife was all right and that he really did have a son.

When he got back Rose was getting breakfast. I'm just taking Pat up a cup of tea," she said. "Could you see to Heather?"

Heather was pouring milk over a mountain of cereal in a bowl.

"Hey there, young lady, what's all the rush?"

"Nana said we could see the baby today. Can I take him a present? Would he like a teddy?"

"Just slow down. We'll go and choose a present at Chantelle's after breakfast – but you still have school this morning. Nana is taking us to the hospital this afternoon. You have to remember that babies need to sleep a lot so don't get too excited."

The three of them arrived at the hospital just before four o'clock. Rose had a small bag of clothes and Bernard had a card he had made himself. Heather had chosen a soft toy – a blue rabbit.

"I've got a white one, just like that," she'd told Chantelle.

"I'm sure the baby will love it," said Chantelle. "Give Katie my love, please, Bernard."

"I will," he had promised. "I can't wait to see her."

Now he was walking into the ward it was as if the other occupants faded into the background. He was vaguely aware of curtains, and groups of people, but his attention was fixed on the woman he loved.

Katie was sitting up in bed looking pale but happy. She reached out and he bent over to hug her, kissing her fervently on the cheek.

There was a chair by the side of the bed and he sat down, holding her hand, waiting for her to speak.

"He's over there, Ned. He's lovely," she said.

He tried to focus on the other side of the bed. Heather and Rose were bending over a plastic crib.

"I'll look in a minute," he said. "How are you?"

"I'm fine. Mum was right. It took less than an hour. He's long, Ned, twenty two inches. He'll be tall."

"He's opened his eyes, Mummy. Can I give him my present?"

Katie turned to her daughter. "Oh, Heather. Let me see. That's his first toy. He won't be able to play with it yet but we'll take it home for him. It's lovely, darling."

"Does he cry?"

"He hasn't done much, yet. Babies only cry when they're hungry."

"When will he be hungry?"

"Not yet. Why don't you go and get yourself a drink from the machine?"

"I'll take her, love," said Rose. "He's beautiful, darling. Well done."

Bernard watched them go, Heather doing a little hop and a jump and Rose trying to keep hold of her hand.

He turned to look at his wife but she was staring at the cot.

He walked round the bed and peered at his son. His eyes were like Katie's, dark and wide, and he had a few wisps of dark brown hair. His nose was long and thin and he was waving his tiny hands.

"His face isn't all screwed up like most babies," he said.

"No. He's handsome," said Katie proudly. "And he's quiet. I think he's going to have a calm nature. Aren't we lucky, Ned?"

Bernard could not put into words the mixture of feelings that having a son had stirred up in him. He was pleased, of course, and proud, but he couldn't admit he was more than a little afraid.

"I'm lucky to have you," he said, returning to her side. "I'll be glad when you are back home."

"Go on, you've hardly had time to miss me."

Bernard didn't reply. He just held her hand, drawing strength from the connection.

"We can't just call him Baby," Katie said once they were home, and the infant was sleeping in his cot. "We're going to have to agree on a name."

They had been trying out various possibilities before

the birth but hadn't decided on any of them.

"What do you think he looks like?" asked Rose.

"I think he's a Robert. Then, if he's not happy with what we called him, he can be Bob or Rob."

"Bob Longman," said Bernard. "I like it."

"And a longer middle name," suggested Rose. "How about Adrian? I've always liked that name."

"Robert Adrian Longman. It sounds quite grand, doesn't it?" Katie giggled.

"He'll be Little Bob for some time, I shouldn't wonder. Heather, would you like your brother to be called Bob?"

"Oh, yes. He's like Bob the Builder isn't he?"

The adults laughed. It hadn't occurred to them but it seemed like a good omen.

James timed it so that Bernard would have returned from taking Heather to school and then knocked gently at the back door. Sandy started to bark. Bernard hurried to put her in the lobby and then opened the door to James.

"It's a boy, then? Can I see him?"

"Bernard, go up and see if it's OK with Katie," said Rose. "Come in, James, have some tea."

"I brought a bottle – we could open it?"

"Later, perhaps."

James put the bottle of whisky down on the kitchen worktop and followed Rose into the dining room.

They heard Bernard coming down the stairs and Rose stepped forward eagerly as he entered the room. Well, Bernard?"

"Katie says give her twenty minutes. She'll be happy to see you then."

"What's his name?" asked James.

"Robert – but he's already Baby Bob."

"That's a good, strong name. I bet you are really proud, Bernie."

"Proud?" said Rose, "He's like the cat that got the cream."

Bernard did not seem to hear. He was searching in a cupboard for something.

"What are you looking for, Bernard?"

"The camera. We must have some pictures."

By the time they had found the camera and James had drunk his tea the time was up and they all climbed the stairs together. The two men hesitated in the doorway, waiting for permission to enter.

"Come in. He's not quite asleep," called Katie. She was sitting up in bed cradling Bob in her arms. His hair was thick and dark and his eyes, which were about to close, were a rich brown, giving him a surprisingly serious expression.

"Do you want to hold him, Ned?" asked Katie.

"Not yet," replied her husband. "He looks settled."

The baby's eyes closed and they all relaxed.

"Just wheel the crib a bit nearer, please, darling, and I'll pop him in."

She laid the baby carefully on his side and pulled up the coverlet.

"He looks like a strong lad," said James, at last.

"He's going to be like his dad," responded Katie and held out her hand to clasp Bernard's.

"I brought the camera," he said.

"Well, you two stay like that and I'll take a picture," said James. "Then I'll take one of Baby Bob. He won't worry about the flash if he's asleep."

The photography over, he made his exit. The whole experience had stirred up memories he'd rather have forgotten. In fact, he felt strangely miserable – as if something was stopping him from fully sharing in their joy. What was the matter with him? It was a question he could not answer.

When he got downstairs Rose was pulling on her coat.

"I'll go and meet Heather. I'm sure Bernard would rather stay with Katie. There's no need to rush off, James."

"No. I'll stay for a bit. Thanks, Rose."

When Bernard came downstairs he looked thoughtful.

"Has Rose gone for Heather?"

"Yes. Is everything OK, Bernie?"

If only he could think of Bernard as a fellow adult – instead of a disabled child – he might be able to connect with his son. He didn't like to see him upset, especially now, when he should be celebrating. What could be wrong?

Bernard was frowning. He seemed to be struggling to put his thoughts into words.

"Not everything. It's Heather. She's so quick. She won't keep still and she brings home a different reading book every day. I wish I could keep up with her, but I can't."

James tried to hide the envy he felt when Bernard boasted about Heather. How different his life would have been if his son had been like that!

"It will be easier when she is at school all day. That will tire her out. She's a credit to you, Bernard. I'm a very lucky grandfather," But somehow he didn't feel like a grandfather. He felt more like a distant cousin, with the emphasis on the word 'distant.'

Two cars slowed by the shop and the passenger jumped out and ran over to the office window.

Rose opened it and leaned forward. "The Hawkins' party?" she asked.

"Yes – Donna and Jane, Mark and Granger – two tents, two cars."

"I'll show you your pitches if you'll just park up by the hedge, please."

Rose studied them as they drove onto the site. They were all in their late teens or early twenties. The girl had sounded local but the boys were dressed in jeans and hooded tops. Why did everyone say hooded tops spelled trouble?

She went through the shop to the camp site.

The youngsters were unpacking their gear and she showed them to the spot she had allotted them near the far gate.

"You've got six tents here already?" asked the girl, looking surprised.

"Yes – but they are all out at present – either walking or down by the sea, I expect."

"How far's the town?" asked one of the boys.

"About three miles, but there is a village less than a mile away in the other direction and a pub within walking distance. The map and the shop hours are all in your introductory pack. I've given one to Donna. I hope you enjoy your stay."

"Can we play football anywhere?" asked the other boy.

"Not here – there's not room – but the village has a recreation ground."

The boy snorted.

"We'll find somewhere," said the second girl. "Come on, let's get on."

She sounded a bit rough, thought Rose, wondering how these four would fit in with the people already on the site.

Next morning it was James who found the answer. First, the newcomers had been drinking until late at night and came back to the site making so much noise that they disturbed most of the people in the other tents. Then they left taps running in the shower room and, if James had not gone out early to check, the place would have been flooded.

Later he saw them kicking a ball about in The Meadows and hoped they would cause no damage. At least no-one was living there yet. He was gearing himself up to speak to them that evening when he found them in the orchard, climbing trees and throwing the immature apples at each other.

"Do you know you are on private property?" he asked.

"What's it to you, Granddad?" sneered one of the boys.

James weighed up his options. He really needed Bernard and Sandy with him.

"Come down now, please, lads. You are ruining the crop."

"Is that your van?" asked the largest boy, menacingly.

"Yes – and I'm going back to it to give you some space. I think the girls would appreciate it if you spent some time with them." Trying to sound more friendly than he felt, he was hoping against hope that the two giggling females would encourage them to move while he was absent.

As soon as he was out of earshot he phoned Lane's End.

"Rose, is Bernard there?"

"Yes. He's in the study."

"Can you ask him to bring Sandy for a walk – but NOT bring anyone else. Those teenage types are getting a bit rowdy."

"I suppose I'll have to ask them to leave. I've never had to do that before."

"Let's give them a chance – perhaps they'll go down to the beach tomorrow. I just wish they were more considerate when they come back at night."

"How about I suggest to the local police that they drive past about midnight just to see that everything is OK?"

"Champion. Tell Bernard the kids are in the orchard – up this end – unless they've done as I asked and come out."

"Oh dear, James, be careful."

"Don't worry. I don't think they'd argue with a dog." But that would only solve the immediate problem. What if they took revenge on his van? His next call was to Brian Sampson.

"Brian – do us a favour, will you? Can two of your boys bring some sleeping bags and kip in the van for the night? I'm just not sure about some of our visitors."

"We'll do better than that. I know someone who'd love to bring his own tent and pitch it between them and you. They won't mess with Charlie."

James phoned Rose to tell her what he had arranged and then went round to Pat's to warn her. Pat was locking up as he arrived.

"I've met those four," she said. "The girls seem bored and I think the boys thought they'd be sleeping with one each, but it hasn't happened so they are at a loose end. I told them about the Bowling Alley and the night clubs but they are too lazy to go any further than the King's Head."

"I'm going to see if they've come out of the orchard," said James. "Bernard is on his way with the dog."

"You know how Sandy is with strange men. I hope there's no trouble. Do you want me to stay?"

"If you like. I'll come and tell you what happens."

James watched as Pat unlocked the door and went inside.

He didn't expect violence but she would be close at hand if anyone did get hurt.

By the time he reached the orchard he knew Bernard had got there before him. Sandy was barking furiously and one of the boys was shouting, "Keep that mutt away from me. If it bites me I'll sue."

"Come down, Mark," said one of the girls. "He's on the lead. He won't hurt you."

"It'd better not try. I'll bash its head in."

Seeing James arrive, the boy slowly began to descend, affecting a deliberate swagger as he reached the ground.

James stood back as the intruders pushed their way through a gap in the hedge and sauntered onto the campsite.

Bernard stayed in the orchard with the excited dog, waiting while James escorted them to their tents.

"I'll just - ?" said the other boy and gestured to the toilets.

"No problem," said James, helpfully. Now they were doing what he had requested there was no need to be officious.

He waited by the gate to the field until everything was quiet and then returned to Bernard. "I've sent for reinforcements," he said, "Brian's boys are staying the night," and as he spoke a pick-up pulled into the car park and a burly figure leaned out.

"Everything quiet?" asked Charlie.

"Sure. They're over the other side, the two tents by Chalk Pit Lane. Thanks, boys. I owe you one."

"Let's just wait and see, shall we?" said his companion. "How about a coffee before we set up?"

"Sure. Do you want one, Bernard?"

"No thanks. I'll say goodnight to Pat and get back to the house. See you in the morning."

That evening the four troublemakers went out through the gate to Chalk Pit Lane as they had the night before, but by ten o'clock the boys were back. They packed their tent into one of the cars and drove off, the bass thumping. An hour later the girls returned, giggling and entered their tent.

There was a loud shriek and they tumbled out into the darkness. Charlie and his mate darted out of their tent and grabbed the hysterical girls.

"What is it?" asked Charlie.

"A snake," cried one. "There's a snake in the tent!"

Charlie brought out a flashlight and pulled back the flap of the tent. Sure enough, what looked like a long, fat snake was stretched out over the sleeping bag. It glistened in the light.

"It's not real. You should have known that. It's all damp," said Charlie.

"How was I supposed to know? I just touched it and

it felt horrible." She was still shaking.

"Where's the boys?" the other man asked.

"They've gone," said Jane. "They said the country was too dull and they knew somewhere they would have more fun."

"You look cold, girls," said Charlie. "How about a nightcap?"

"Is that your tent?" asked Donna.

"Yes. It's a big one, isn't it?" and Charlie laughed.

"Well, as you saved us, thanks. We'd love to, wouldn't we, Jane?"

Jane nodded and the pair followed Charlie to his tent.

James watched from the window of his campervan. That seemed like a satisfactory conclusion.

Summer promised to be busy with visitors. Heather blossomed as families she knew from previous years came to stay at the campsite. When Lisa and John brought Ryan for a week she and her mother could not have been happier.

Then, one day, as Katie was wheeling Robert out of the clinic Tania shouted at her from across the road. "Have you heard?" Tania panted as she ran up to her.

"What now?"

"It's Tony. He's dead. He committed suicide."

"Jessica's Tony? Oh, no! What happened?"

"He's been moping about the house on his own for weeks. He looked a mess, Katie, but he wouldn't let anyone help him. I tried to get him to call Jessica's parents in Torquay. I don't know if he ever did – but last night he went down to the level crossing and ran in front of a train."

"The selfish idiot – was anyone else hurt?"

"The driver was shocked and people were bruised but nothing major. The line is still closed. Isn't it horrible?"

But Katie had stopped listening. "I should have realised he was sick. A fine care worker I am!" she said at last. "When Jessica came to us and told us how her husband behaved I should have guessed. Oh, Tania, if I'd got professional help I might have been able to stop him."

"You know where Jessica is?"

"Yes. We'll have to tell her before it's in the papers."

"Where's she gone?"

"Not far – but she's changed, Tania. I don't know how she'll take it."

"Be pleased, most like."

"Don't say that. He was still the twins' father. I'll ring her."

"Tell her I'd like to meet up sometime."

"I will. I must get back now, be seeing you, Tania." Katie felt sick but she couldn't vomit in the street. She swallowed hard and pushed her shoulders back. What dreadful news on such a lovely sunny day. How could she break it to her friend?

When she arrived home she tried the farm phone. She didn't want to talk to Jess if she was busy. "Is Jess there, please?"

"Yes. I'll fetch her. Who is it?"

"It's Katie." She waited until her friend picked up the receiver.

"Hallo, Katie. What's up?"

"I've got some bad news, Jess. Is it all right to talk? I didn't know when you were working and I wanted to talk to you when the twins weren't around."

"I'm listening. Is it the baby?"

"No, he's fine. It's Tony."

"What's he done now?" There was a sigh in her voice.

"I'm afraid he's dead."

"He's what?"

"He's dead. I'm sorry, Jess. I should have come over. I just didn't feel up to driving."

"No-no, I'm all right. I just can't believe it. Did someone kill him?"

"No. I'm afraid he killed himself."

"I might have known. How?"

"He ran in front of a train."

"The thoughtless brute. Did anyone else get hurt? How did you find out?"

"Tania told me. It only happened last night."

"I'll come back. Things will need sorting out. I can leave the twins here for a few days. I've still got a key for the front door. I'll get in touch when I know what's going on. I suppose the police will want to speak to me, and a doctor." She was gabbling frantically.

"Try the hospital – they'll tell you what to do. If you need help, Jess, let us know."

"You've got plenty on your plate – but thanks for telling me. I might have known this wouldn't last."

Katie put down the phone. What a sad reaction to her husband's death. No-one ever knows what goes on between married couples, she thought, and you just can't predict the future.

14

I t was nearly the end of August when Katie marched through the orchard, pushing the pram. Usually the trip to the clinic was a happy formality but today her face was like thunder.

"Targets!" she spat out as she put the brake on the pram and stormed indoors. "Bloody check-lists. Tick boxes! Weight, eyes, ears, smiles - if you aren't the same as everyone else there's something wrong! I HATE being compared and cross-examined."

"Who's comparing you?" Rose hadn't seen her daughter so angry for months.

"Not me – Bob. He doesn't fit their pattern – doesn't respond as they'd expect. He's only a couple of months old – babies aren't robots!"

"Give it time. Boys are always slower than girls. Don't let it upset you."

"He's not overweight like some of them and he doesn't squeal all the time. Oh – it makes me so mad!"

"He's a happy baby. That's all that matters."

But it wasn't.

Katie went alone to Tony's funeral.

Jess wore black, a sombre skirt with a white blouse, but the change in her was obvious. Her hair was short and stylish and she carried herself more confidently, almost proudly. The twins seemed different too – their faces brown from being outside and their natural exuberance confined for the occasion like a lidded pan of boiling water.

There were no tears. Tony had no other relatives present and very few people stayed for refreshments after the service.

Katie followed Jessica into the kitchen. The house had a sad, neglected, feel. It was clean, of course, but the carpets were worn and the furniture obviously second hand.

"Are you going to be OK, Jess?" she asked.

"Oh, yes. Tony and I wrote our wills when we bought the house twelve years ago. The place is mine, Katie, but I'm going to sell it. I'm going to look for somewhere near the farm."

"How's the business going?"

"Great."

"You never did study reflexology, then?"

"No. That wasn't really practical. I employ three people now. Fancy that – me - a boss!"

"I'm pleased for you, and you've given me an idea."

"What's that?"

"I need a different job, one I can do from home. While Rose is still with us I'd like to re train."

"But you already have qualifications."

"Only in caring for the elderly. I don't want to do that for the rest of my life. I thought I'd try chiropody."

"I see – feet again!" Jess laughed.

"That's what I mean. You gave me the idea. I've already done similar work at the care home. I know what to expect – but I could travel about and choose my own hours. I'm sure it would work."

"How much do they charge?"

"I don't know – but I'm going to look into it. It just seems the right time to change."

As the months passed and Bob showed no sign of reaching expected milestones the family became more and more concerned.

"When did you crawl? When did you say something?" Katie would demand of Bernard.

"I don't remember. Ask James."

But James was rarely about. He seemed to be avoiding Lane's End. His van was still on the site but he seemed to be working long hours and did not answer his phone.

He'd spent Christmas day with them but he'd been very quiet.

Heather had a new doll that cried real tears and spoke, with lots of clothes to dress her in, but even her antics did not seem to stop him brooding.

The weather worsened and, for a while, they were forced to stay indoors. Pat closed the shop for the whole of February and the family almost hibernated.

Then, in early March, Rose went down to the camp site and the campervan was gone.

Thinking that perhaps James had needed it to transport something she waited until later in the day and checked again. It was still missing.

She raced round to the shop to see Pat.

"I don't know about James," said her sister-in law, "but Chantelle left an envelope for you. I found it when I opened up."

Rose took the envelope and opened it. Inside she found a letter and a cheque for a month's rent.

Dear Rose, it began. *Sorry to leave you so suddenly but James was in a hurry to get to a new job he's been offered. I hope this will tide you over until the spring, Yours, Chantelle.*

"What does she mean, James was in a hurry?" gasped Rose.

"They must have gone together."

"What? James and Chantelle? He's almost 30 years older than her!"

"Yes, but you must admit they did get on."

"Get on! I'll give him get on! No note from him, I suppose. What a coward – what an absolute coward."

She sat down suddenly, shaking and putting her hand to her eyes to stop the tears.

"Come into the office, Rose. I'll make some tea."

"I can't go on, Pat. It's too much for me. We owe money all over the place. I need to sell up."

"Did you know Katie had her eye on one of the new houses?"

"No. She didn't tell me."

"I think she was waiting to see if you could help with the deposit."

"She'd better get a move on. They're going up for sale next month."

"I think she might have an arrangement with Brian. She and James had something cooking."

"Seems to me he had too much cooking," Rose snarled.

"Ask her. I don't think she'll mind that James and Chantelle have gone."

Rose challenged Katie as soon as she saw her. "What's this about the new houses?"

"Oh, that. I really wanted one but it's reserved. We couldn't afford it, anyway."

"Yes, you could – if I sell Lane's End. I'll see to it straight away. I don't know why I was waiting and now this has happened I'm certain."

"Now what has happened?"

"James – he's gone off with Chantelle."

"I don't believe it. He's old enough to be her father."

"I know that – you know that, but the silly girl must have been besotted."

"That's another rent lost. First Mike and then Chantelle."

"And Pat took nothing for a month – we can't go on like this, Katie."

"What are we going to do?"

"Zak has been working behind the scenes. He thinks if the garden centre people demolish the house we might have a good case to turn the shop into a residence. We wouldn't be allowed to change the outside but if the Parish Council supports us it could just get permission."

"How long would all that take?"

"Normally six months at least – but the garden centre people have all their plans ready. They were just waiting for me to accept their offer."

"You mean we could be in this year?"

"Well, in the new house. You'd have to put me up for a few months until my place was ready. It all depends on planning permission."

"It won't be much fun round here while they are

building the Garden Centre."

"No – but think how handy it will be when it's finished. They'll probably have a coffee shop, and probably some work for Bernard."

"Mum, it's a great idea. If only the house I wanted hadn't been reserved."

"You'd better get in touch with Mr Sampson and let him know you want one of the others."

"I will – now."

"What do you want with two houses?" said Brian Sampson when Katie rang.

"I don't want two. I wanted number ten but it's reserved."

"Of course it's reserved. It's reserved for you."

"How?"

"James. Your father-in-law paid a deposit as soon as it was completed. He said it was the least he could do. Ask him."

"I can't. He's gone, but is it all legal?"

"Signed, sealed and delivered. You can move in when you're ready."

Katie was dumbfounded. After hearing her mother rail against James and recognising that not only was she angry that he had betrayed their trust, but was also hurt because she thought they had an understanding, she was ready to dismiss him as a charming sponger. Now he had shown a generous side of his nature that was entirely unexpected. How could she ever thank him? He'd never given any indication that he had money. Where did it come from? Was he some kind of fraudster or crook? Could they accept such a large amount from someone they didn't really know?

"He did consider himself family, you know," said Pat, when she tried to explain to her how she felt.

"Why didn't he stay?"

"I think he was scared. He'd become so fond of Heather and so happy with you all and then Bob was born and all his old doubts returned."

"But Bob is so little, and he doesn't even look like Ned."

"Who know what goes on inside someone else's head? I don't even know what Chantelle thought she was doing."

"I do – escaping. She had a tough life with those parents of hers. They doted on her brother because he was a soldier and away fighting, while they treated her like a slave."

"We'll miss them both. What will Bernard say? I don't know which of them he will miss most."

He doesn't even look like Ned. Katie's words echoed in her head. Bob looked like her, didn't he? Yet the deep brown eyes reminded her of Al. She tried to bury the thought.

She needed to do something physical. She felt like cutting and chopping but all she could think of was picking some daffodils and taking them to the King's Head. They said they'd like to have some fresh flowers for the tables. She needed to be out, away from the family. She had a letter to post and then she needed time to think.

How could she tell her husband his father had gone, again? Would it be better to let Rose do it? She didn't want Ned to think she was being spiteful.

The letter was addressed to Mr J. Mann and was in Katie's handwriting.

James felt uncomfortable opening it front of Chantelle. The message was short.

Dear James, she wrote, *Thank you very much for helping us to buy the house. It was very generous of you. I'm sorry you did not feel able to say goodbye and I hope you make each other happy. Our best wishes to Chantelle,*

Yours, Katie.

How could he have said goodbye? he thought. How could he have faced Bernard? He could never have justified his actions to Rose, or Bernard. He only knew that being with them, and watching Bob grow up, was like going back in time, to when he had hated himself, his wife and everything in his life. He couldn't bear to go through that again.

He handed the letter to Chantelle.

He hadn't planned to take her with him. He'd asked her out for a meal at the King's Head to say goodbye.

She'd sat there pouring out her heart to him, explaining how she couldn't wait for the Garden Centre to open. She wasn't making enough money to pay the rent on the shop and without it she had nothing.

He'd watched as she ate her pasta, her stole slipping from her shoulders, her creamy skin tempting him. He'd tried to concentrate on his steak.

"How's yours?" she asked, between mouthfuls.

"Fine – and you've chosen a wine I like."

"Mum and Dad are into wine. It seems to help them get on better."

"You don't like living at home, do you, Chantelle?"

"What's there to like? Mum thinks she's the leading light of the local amateur operatic society but she's past it and no-one dare tell her. Dad sits on the Parish Council and acts as if he's the Prime Minister. Kevin is only home once in a blue moon and all he can talk about is the army – and I'm the only one who cares what the house looks like or what we are going to eat."

"Do you do all the cooking?"

"No. Mum makes puddings sometimes. Otherwise we have cake. I tried to introduce fresh fruit but the pears went sleepy and no-one would touch the apples. I like grapes but I eat them with cheese and biscuits." She looked down at her lap and shrugged. "I guess I just like food."

"I think it's probably genetic," said James. "but it suits you. I like your style."

"Don't let's talk about me. What's all this in aid of?"

James had almost forgotten the purpose of the date. How could he tell her he was leaving when she was so obviously enjoying the evening? How could he tell her at all? The one person he could not bear to leave was Chantelle.

When Victor had rung and asked if he was coming back for the summer season he felt that he had found the answer of how to break free from all that held him to the family at Lane's End. He'd felt things changing and the demands on him increasing.

He was guardian of the camp site, advisor to Katie, still a stranger to Bernard, and just another adult to Heather. He'd hoped to be able to give his granddaughter the love and attention he had denied his son but there were too many other people with a stronger claim on her attention, and the new baby just reminded him of Bernard.

They were a unit without him. They understood each other in a way he never would. Within the family Bernard was accepted, loved, appreciated even, whereas all James saw were his son's deficiencies.

They didn't need him. Rose might think she did. He was afraid to put into words what it was he thought she wanted from him. Whatever it was – it was too much, and now was his opportunity to get away.

Chantelle finished her meal and was looking at him expectantly.

"Coffee?" he asked, delaying the inevitable.

"James. You are acting very oddly," chided his companion. "Is it bad news or good news?"

"I've got to go away," he blurted out.

"How long for?"

He was staring at her lovely open face. He wanted to kiss it. He didn't want to see her cry. "I don't know," he prevaricated. "Could you come with me?"

"Where to?"

"The Lake District. I used to help out at an outdoor store every summer. They've missed me. They want me to go back."

"And you want to go?"

"Yes. I don't belong here."

"Everyone has loved having you around."

"Perhaps – but there's only one person I would miss – and that's you, Chantelle. What do you say?"

"As your girl friend?"

It hadn't occurred to James. He didn't know what he was suggesting. He knew he did not want to get married again but he didn't want to be parted from her.

"Would you stay in the van with me if we weren't married?" he asked, dreading the reply.

Chantelle gave a sigh. "James, if I could be with you I wouldn't care if we were married or not."

He couldn't believe what he was hearing. She was

talking as if she cared about him and he hadn't even realised she felt that way. He reached across the table and clasped her hand.

"I've just lost my appetite," he said, "Shall we go back to my place?"

Her face changed, then, and she looked round to se if anyone was watching them.

"I daren't," she said. "If I stayed out all night my parents would call the police. If you take me home now I can pack a few things and meet you in the morning, really early."

"I'll drive the van up to the church and meet you there, about six?"

She giggled as he paid for the meal and then draped her coat round her shoulders. He could not resist a swift peck on her neck and was amazed when, further along the road, she rewarded him with a loving embrace.

How he'd missed the feel of a woman next to him. He couldn't believe he had wasted so much time. There was so much about Chantelle that he admired and he could hardly believe that someone like her could be happy to make a life with him.

But she was, they were together, and life was so good he wanted to savour every second.

She read the letter in silence. "We did do the right thing, didn't we, James?"

"Darling, they will be happy, I'm sure of it," and he took her in his arms, holding on to the moment as if he feared it would not last.

"Bernard, did you know James liked Chantelle?" asked Rose in the evening.

"He was always round there. She made him laugh."

"Well, when your father was offered another job he decided to take Chantelle with him."

"Is it far away? When are they going?"

"I'm afraid they've gone."

Bernard seemed to freeze. All the animation left his face and his brows closed together and his teeth clenched. Eventually he opened his mouth and took a deep breath – shaking his shoulders as he did so. "He's run away, again?"

"Yes."

"And he didn't say goodbye?"

"No."

"I never, ever, want to see him again," and he stomped off up the stairs.

Hearing the shouting, Bob started to cry.

"I'll see to him, mum," said Katie. "We'd better not mention the house until Ned's calmed down."

"I've never seen him so angry," said Rose. "How that man could treat us like that I just don't know."

Bernard seemed to sink into a pit of despair. He walked in a daze, picked at his food, hardly spoke a word and would only change his clothes when Katie insisted. It was almost as if he didn't want to live any more. The only thing that brought a fleeting smile to his lips was Bob, and Katie was content to let him share the care of their son.

She had returned to work, but on an early shift so that she could spend evenings with Heather. Most days she collected her from school and heard all about her day and even went with her sometimes to visit friends. It was nice feeling like the other mums, although she kept away from those with new babies. They were just too competitive.

The new houses were selling fast – at least, the two bed roomed ones were. The semi detached with three and four bedrooms had only two allotted.

Some evenings she would take Sandy and wander round the little Close, staring at the house that was to be their new home – trying to imagine the rooms as she would have them, the furniture and furnishings.

Rose and Katie had decided they shouldn't tell Bernard about it until they were certain Lane's End was sold. It seemed to be taking such a long time. They had heard there had been objections from someone in the village – but the company had met all the planning requirements. The main entrance was to be from Stable Lane. Chalk Pit Lane was too narrow, but it could still be used for deliveries. Some of the orchard would have to go to make room for a car park – but there would be a screen of trees between the campsite and the centre.

The company finally exchanged contracts in September and, with Christmas creeping up on them, the family needed to be told.

They were all gathered together in the lounge. Katie and Ned were sitting on the settee, Bob was asleep and Heather had her nose in a book.

Rose began the conversation. "That wasn't such a good crop, this year, was it, Bernard?" she said.

"No. We need new trees."

"And no-one has taken the units. I think we'll have to sell up."

Bernard looked alarmed.

Knowing how content Bernard had been at Lane's End Rose looked to Katie for support.

"If we sell this place where will we go?" he said. He turned to Katie and she took his hand and said calmly,

"That's what we need to talk about. We've put a deposit on one of the houses in The Meadows."

Bernard looked as if he was struggling to accept the idea. Eventually he said, "Which one?"

"Number ten."

"The big one at the back?"

"Yes. We can move in as soon as we like."

"Before we sell Lane's End?"

"Yes. We should be able to have Christmas there."

Bernard didn't ask where the money had come from – and they didn't tell him. Katie was just happy that, at last, he seemed interested in something.

"I can plan the garden," he murmured. "Can we go and look at it now?"

Katie laughed, "Of course – let's all go – we can decide who sleeps where and what colours we want. Come on, Heather – we are going to see our new house."

"I don't want a new house. I want to stay here."

"Well, come and see it, anyway. There's a room for you and a room for Bob and you will be near Auntie Pat and nearer your school friends."

"Can I show Oliver?"

"Yes – when we've got it finished. You can come to town on Saturday and pick some material for curtains. Oh, I've waited so long for this."

She led the way while Ned wheeled the still sleeping baby through the orchard and across the road.

Heather sullenly dragged her feet, but eventually curiosity got the better of her and she counted the numbers on the houses.

"You've got a key, already?" asked Bernard.

"Yes – but I didn't want to go inside without you." She pushed open the door and they stepped into the hallway. Rose took Bob out of his pram and carried him inside.

"It's cold in here, Mummy," said Heather.

"Yes – but we won't use the heating until we move in."

"It's all the same colour," said Bernard, moving from the hall to the kitchen.

"You can fix that. I like the white doors. I thought we'd leave the hall cream, have a green dining room and a pale mushroom sitting room."

"This is a big room," commented Rose, following her daughter and Heather.

"Yes – and I love the French doors out into the garden."

"There's a conservatory off the kitchen. The little houses haven't got that," called out Bernard.

"And we've got a garage – but there's only room for one car." She turned to Rose.

"That's fine – don't forget there's a car park across the road for the camping site."

"Can we go upstairs?" asked Heather.

"The big room is ours but you can choose one of the others," replied her mother.

They followed the youngster as she explored the little room at the front and the two rooms next to the bathroom.

"I like this one," she said at last.

"It's not as big as the others."

"But I like seeing the road, not the garden."

"That's because there's nothing in the garden," laughed Rose. "You might change your mind when it is full of plants and birds."

"I won't. Daddy, can I have wallpaper? Karen has

wallpaper with pictures on."

"Well, that's a change from pink," said Katie. "I'm sure we can find some. What do you think, Ned?"

Bernard had wandered into the largest bedroom and was staring out across the garden to the fields beyond. "That's where the river is, where we found the horse," he mused.

"This is a lovely view."

"We are going to be happy here, aren't we, Ned?" Katie came up behind him and put her arms around him.

"I hope so," he said, wistfully.

Rose was still carrying Bob and had stopped in the next room. "This is your room, Bob," she was saying to the baby,

"And I'll be next door until I can get my own place. That will suit me, right next to the bathroom."

"Can we get it done by Christmas?" asked Katie.

"Not all of it," replied Rose, "But we can start, can't we, Bernard?"

Bernard did not reply. He led them back down the stairs.

"No holiday for us this year," said Katie. "I've got so much to tell Lisa."

Rose sat Bob down on the imitation wood floor in the sitting room. The baby looked round for something to play with and, spotting Bernard's shoes, leaned forward to touch them. He was too far away so he pushed and wriggled on his backside until he could reach the laces.

"Did you see that, Mum?" crowed Katie. "He might not be crawling yet but he's beginning to get about."

"Yes – he'll be into everything before you know it. There's so much space here – it's wonderful, love."

Bernard picked up his son and swung him over his head.

"Bob, boy – you are going to love it here," he said and the baby chuckled.

Katie watched as her husband put Bob over his shoulder. If a new baby and a new house didn't break him out of his depression she didn't know what would. He didn't have dreams and plans for the future like she did. He had no desire to change his life. He just took what fate dished out to him and either suffered or accepted. She wanted so much to make him happy. If only he could share the joy and hope she was feeling now.

15

Rose stood alone in the empty shell of the place that had been her home for over sixty years. She could almost imagine what the two cottages had looked like before they had been knocked together – the large downstairs rooms, the toilets out the back and the bare, chilly bedrooms. A piece of history was about to be destroyed.

She wouldn't come back. She didn't want to see it being demolished. "I'm sorry, Dad," she said to herself. It looked shabby, now, and dark, compared with the new house, Katie's new house. She would never feel anything but a lodger in The Meadows.

Even if she couldn't turn the shop into a home she would find an alternative. She might even buy a motorhome and park it where James's van had been.

The thought of James made her wince. She'd been a romantic old fool, hadn't she? He'd made her feel so special – but then he did that with everyone, didn't he? Everyone except Bernard.

Poor Bernard. Leaving Lane's End was offering her freedom and time to do whatever she liked, go wherever she wished, but for Bernard it had seemed to be a disaster.

Still, the letter she had opened this morning could change everything.

She had, at first, been reluctant to open it. The contents would decide what she should do with the rest of her life.

If it was good news she could start to plan her new home – but if the Council had refused permission to change the shop into a dwelling she would have to stay at the Meadows.

Still, she did have a plan. It would involve a lot of work but it could solve Bernard's problems.

The contents of the letter were short and to the point. Permission had been refused. It was considered likely that, at some stage, the Garden Centre might want to expand and a residence on the land would prevent that.

Also the village envelope contained enough houses, with none now beyond the chalk pit, and a single home there would create a precedent. The building could, however, continue to be used for sales or leisure use.

That last sentence made her smile. Thank goodness they had built showers and toilets when they turned the stables into units.

Now she would have to find someone who knew about indoor play schemes. She would turn the shop into a play area for children – one they could use in bad weather. Then the place could be occupied all year round instead of only in the summer.

She would also look into her other option, a mobile home, one she could live in on site, but also use for travelling around the country.

She smiled to herself. It was almost as if she'd hoped for that decision. She didn't mean it to look as if she wanted to leave the family but, to be honest, she was content with the way things had turned out.

Bernard had left Bob in his playpen with his toy farm. Bob was driving the tractor over a cushion and making engine noises.

Bernard was sitting at the table carefully composing a letter.

Zak had promised to come and connect him to something called Broadband. He didn't know what it was but he hadn't felt the need to use the computer since they had moved.

Now Heather could read so well by herself the sense of urgency to help her had gone.

It was Bob who took up his time now and he was happy that Rose had thought up a plan that would suit his son and himself.

DEAR ZAK he wrote.
THE NEW HOUSE IS FINE.
THE SHED IS IN THE GARDEN.
ROSE SAID SHE WILL HAVE A PLAYING
ROOM IN THE UNITS LIKE A PARK.
I AM LOOKING IN HEATHERS BOOKS
TO SEE WORDS.
I NO apple and happy.
SEE YOU SOON.   BERNARD.

It didn't seem much but he'd done it without help. He copied the address onto the envelope. Zak had told him he would teach them all to e-mail but he was content with the old fashioned system, especially as Zak always wrote in capitals.

Bernard tied Sandy up outside the pet shop and wheeled Bob inside. The pushchair was so handy for carrying large bags of dog food. He made his purchases and turned to see Bob sitting forward in the chair – reaching out to a low cage.

"Bunny," he called, "Bunny."

He was right. A fat white rabbit sat calmly nibbling a carrot. Bernard felt elated.

He'd been the first to witness Bob's first word. How could such a small action give him so much pleasure?

Even as he had the thought another pushed its way into his consciousness.

Had his father ever felt like that about him? He thought not. He had the feeling his mother had hugged all signs of progress to herself. He felt tempted to do the same – but that wouldn't be fair on Katie.

No- he would never treat Bob the way his parents had treated him. He certainly would not be anything like James. Nothing would make him desert his wife and child.

He looked at the beaming face of his son. One day- in spite of having to keep them off the vegetables – he'd get a 'bunny' for Robert.

He distracted him with a new ball for Sandy, on a rope this time, and managed to get outside without any fuss.

Walking home, he was still wondering whether to tell anyone what the boy had said.

It gave him a warm feeling, knowing something the

others didn't.

Watching Heather learn so quickly had been depressing him.

He still wanted to read like other people, even without Chantelle to help him, but the smarter Heather appeared the less he felt like making the effort.

He'd be a baby-sitter for a time, at least while Katie was doing her course, but what then? Would he ever find the satisfaction he'd had while tending the market garden?

Katie watched Ned, Bob and Sandy playing in the garden. She wasn't jealous this time.

They might have a wordless connection but it balanced out because Heather had grown to depend on her, and she was satisfied with that.

She enjoyed all the stories her daughter told her, although she had the feeling her daughter exaggerated for dramatic effect.

She looked down at the letter she was writing to Lisa, wondering if her friend knew what an important part of her life she had become. Everything she could not tell her mother or Ned she poured into her letters to Lisa.

Dear Lisa,

Thank you for the Christmas card. It was great to hear all your news. I am so glad Ryan got into the football team. John always hoped he'd be sporty, didn't he? I hope John enjoys his new job and congratulations on your promotion.

The new house is wonderful. I have a big double oven and a washing machine and tumble drier and a dishwasher that Mum refuses to use and Ned has wallpapered Heather's room in beautiful paper covered in fairies. Heather's choice!

We had an argument about the chickens but in the end they went to Jessica's friends at the farm. I just didn't want that sort of garden. Ned did bring the cherry tree and the new shed but he's dreading the time when they start digging up the apple trees.

The course is fine. Chiropody is so much more than cutting nails and treating corns and the other people with me are so friendly. I really feel a new woman.

Heather is also sporty. Mum takes her to dance classes every Saturday but I think she is just waiting for the summer when she can show what she can do in the school sports day. She won't walk anywhere. She's always running.

The units are all full of Mum's stuff. She's acting really weird – like a sort of temporary housekeeper. I think leaving Lane's End affected her more than she expected it to. Having money doesn't make you happy – it just gives you more to worry about. Still, as long as we don't get another flood we'll be OK. and if we did , we'd be protected by the other houses.

We haven't yet got used to having neighbours. A middle-aged couple have moved in next door but I haven't spoken to them yet. I wonder what they would think if we told them they lived in Un-Stable Lane!

Perhaps we could come up and see you in the holidays. I think it would make a change to see the east coast. I've got a bigger car now we have to take Bob with us when we go out. Mum has plans to make the camping site more child friendly. I hope they work out because Ned needs a new project. It's funny, but we all miss Chantelle more than James.

You know, there was a time when I thought she was getting too friendly with Ned. How stupid was that?

Heather is back, now – hungry, as usual, so I'd better finish.

Love, Katie.

They were all together, sitting round the table, when Bernard told them.

Robert was in his high chair, between Bernard and Rose, and Katie was dishing up the meal. The steak and kidney pie looked and smelled enticing.

Bernard realised how hungry his walk had made him.

Rose was carefully pouring gravy onto some potato and making sure there were no lumps in the mashed swede.

"Robert said 'Bunny' while we were at the pet shop," declared Bernard. "He must have seen it was the same as his toy."

"That's marvellous," said Katie, looking as if she didn't really believe him.

"I'll get Fluffy and see if he'll do it again," said Heather, starting to get up.

"You sit still," said her mother. "There's plenty of time for that. There's no need to let your meal get cold."

Rose dug a spoon into the potato and offered it to Bob. He leaned forward eagerly and sucked happily at the contents while they all began to eat.

"I got twenty out of twenty for my spelling test," said Heather. "Donna got recipe wrong."

"That always used to catch me out," said Rose, offering Robert a spoonful of mashed swede.

Robert's little face crumpled at the taste and the orange mush dripped from his mouth.

"Hey, little one, it's good for you," said Katie. "Put some gravy on it, Mum. He might like it, then."

Rose dropped the next spoonful of swede into the gravy and offered it to her grandson, but before it reached his mouth Robert waved his arms and shouted, "No."

They all watched as he turned his head away from the

approaching spoon.

Katie burst out giggling. "What was the first word you heard your son say?" she intoned and then replied, in her own voice, "No." and they all laughed.

"Make him say it again, Nana," said Heather.

"Not now," said Katie, "He might not eat the rest of his dinner – but it does show he is listening to us. You were right, Ned, at last he's beginning to talk."

The letter they found on the mat in the morning was postmarked Keswick.

"It's for you, Bernard," said Rose, "Shall I read it?"

"Yes, please."

Before she could open the letter a photograph dropped out of the envelope. It was a picture of James and Chantelle – standing on the crest of a hill, arms entwined. On the back it just said, "The Lakes."

Rose opened the letter and began to read. "It's from Chantelle," she said. "She says she and James have got work in a shop. She hopes we have forgiven her for leaving without telling us and that she would like to keep in touch. James is having trouble with arthritis so he's not doing so much decorating. The address on the top is some kind of store." She paused, and then added, "I do hope he doesn't let her down."

Katie was staring at the photograph. For months, now, the issue of the identity of Bob's father had been haunting her. She knew in her heart of hearts that it had to be Ned, but the older Bob grew the more he looked like Al. It was beginning to make her feel less loving towards him.

Now she gave a sigh of relief. Al wasn't the only man

she knew with strong features. Looking at the photograph of James she could see, if she discounted the colouring, Bob's face shape with its long nose was exactly like his grandfather's.

"I'm not going to worry any more," she told herself. "Robert Adrian Longman - you are very precious and I love you."

Also by Julie Round.

Lane's End 2007